THE BROKEN SOULS

DI RITA GUPTA MURDER MYSTERY

BOOK 4

SAM CARTER

Copyright © 2025 by Sam Carter
All rights reserved.
The right of Sam Carter to be identified as the author of this work has been asserted by him in accordance with the Copyright, Designs and Patents Act 1988.
No part of this book may be reproduced in any form or by any electronic or mechanical means, including information storage and retrieval systems, without permission in writing from the author. Infringement of copyright by copying.
(1) The copying of the work is an act restricted by the copyright in every description of copyright work and references in this part to copying and copies shall be construed as follows.
(2) Copying in relation to a literary, dramatic, musical, or artistic work means reproducing the work in any material form.
This includes storing the work in any medium by electronic means.
(3) Copying in relation to the typographical arrangement of a published edition means making a facsimile copy of the arrangement.
(4) Copying in relation to any description of work includes the making of copies that are transient or are incidental to some other use of the work.
This book is a work of fiction. Names, characters, places, and incidents either are
products of the author's imagination or are used fictitiously. Any resemblance to actual
persons, living or dead, events, or locales is entirely coincidental.

CHAPTER 1

A stiff wind blew in from the cliffs facing the North Sea.

Rachel grabbed Ethan's hand as the breeze cut across the promenade of South Beach. The tide was up, waters lapping against the stones. The row of streetlights curved around the bay, shimmering in the night like a garland. Their light cast yellow cones on the restless, dark waters. It was pretty, Rachel thought, but she wanted the wind to die down. She snuggled closer to Ethan, who put an arm around her shoulder.

They had had a few drinks at the bars in town, but Scarborough was quiet, and the sea was calling. They had just been to the town center and done a pub crawl. They ended up in a DJ bar, where Ethan started ordering shots of rum, and they got really drunk.

It was September now, and with the schools open, the crowds had gone.

The beach looked beautiful, she thought. The sky was a deep velvet blue, and she could see the faint, dark outline of the cliffs that jutted out into the sea. Rachel looked to her left, where the houses facing the sea were brightly lit. Beyond them, looming on the hills, the lights of Scarborough Castle glimmered faintly. She wished they would put more lights on the castle ramparts. She tugged on Ethan's arm.

"We should go up to the castle at night. The views must be great."

"Yes. Better than going into town, let's face it."

Rachel agreed. Scarborough town had too many boarded-up shop windows.

"We should go to Bridlington," she said. "It's nicer."

Ethan nodded and pulled on Rachel's hand, heading for the beach.

"Come on. Let's go for a quick swim."

Rachel giggled, then started laughing. She looked up at the sky, with its wide canopy of silver-studded stars. She felt light-headed, warm, and relaxed. The stars swam in her eyes, and when she looked down, the sea crashed and foamed, the waters restless.

She held Ethan's hand tightly. "The tide's up. We could get caught."

"No, it won't be full tide till later in the month." He pointed at the sickle-shaped moon in the sky. "A few more days till that becomes a full circle."

Rachel giggled again, adrenaline battling with caution. The caution was fading fast, and the alcohol was fueling her actions.

Ethan gave her a peck on the cheek. His breath was warm on her skin.

"Come on, it'll be fun. Besides, we can be alone on the beach, right?"

He winked at her, and she felt the heat rising in her cheeks. True, last week they had spent an hour on the beach, where no one could see them. Ethan knew a nice spot, hidden by the rocks, sheltered from the wind. The memory of that night filled Rachel with desire.

He put his arm around her, and they stepped off the promenade onto the sand. The sea breeze wasn't warm at night, not in Scarborough. Rachel was blasted by a gust that sent her hair everywhere. She pulled out her cap and put it on. She was glad to snuggle under Ethan's arm—he was taller than her. The sand made walking difficult, and they picked their way slowly.

Twice, they stumbled on the sand, and then Ethan fell down, with Rachel jumping on top of him. They laughed and play-fought in the sand, then ran as best as they could with their shoes on.

The rocks were near the cliffs, and they weren't far from a big sheltering formation. Rachel sighed in relief when she stepped behind the massive boulder. The wind died down instantly, whining overhead. She stepped over some small rocks, kissed smooth by wind and sand.

Giggling, they stripped down to their underwear. Ethan grabbed her, and they kissed passionately. Rachel felt the warmth of Ethan's skin, and desire pooled low in her belly.

"Come on," Ethan whispered, pulling at her hand.

Rachel laughed, and they ran down the sand into the water. It was freezing cold, and she yelped as the first wave hit her. The ice-cold sting was sobering, as was the whip of the North Sea wind. They splashed around for a while in knee-deep water. Ethan wanted to go deeper, but Rachel wasn't so sure.

After a while, they ran back to the rock formation. The rock formation was a blessing. There was no wind behind the boulders. Rachel shivered as she used Ethan's shirt to dry herself. Ethan would wear his wet shirt until they got back to their hotel, which they could see from here, up on the promontory.

The floor was sandy now, and unexpectedly warm. She dug her feet into it. Then she felt something soft and recoiled immediately. Ethan was behind her, kissing her shoulder.

"Ethan, there's something here."

"What do you mean?"

He came over, hearing the concern in her voice. He pointed his phone light at the ground. It took them a few seconds to realise what they were looking at.

It was like a sandcastle, but as the light tracked upwards, it revealed the full shape. It was a human being, half the body covered in sand, up to waist level. The hands were folded on the chest, and it was a woman. She lay in perfect repose, as if she had gone to sleep. Her black hair spread like a halo around her head.

They gasped, and Rachel couldn't breathe. She clutched Ethan tightly as he moved closer.

The woman's eyes were open wide, staring into nothing. Her chest wasn't moving. Her skin was a pasty white, and she was clearly dead.

Rachel felt the panic crawl up her spine and spread noxious tentacles into her limbs. The horror struck her like a whiplash, and she screamed.

CHAPTER 2

The car hurtled down the dirt track, and Detective Constable Maggie Long's head slammed against the window. She grimaced in pain and held her head. Sweat poured down her face as she looked at the driver, Edward Warren—an evil man who had abducted a little boy and killed his stepfather.

"Kyle… I mean Ed, whatever your name is, stop the car. Please."

Tears budded in Maggie's eyes and trickled down her face. "I'm begging you." She put a hand over her belly. "I'm carrying your child, for heaven's sake."

A crack seemed to appear in Edward's dry, tight face. His lips parted, and the hardness in his jaw relaxed. Then his mouth bent into a snarl, and he gripped the steering wheel tighter. He didn't take his foot off the accelerator.

Maggie cried out as the car lurched into a hole in the dirt track.

Edward steadied the car and shot her a venomous glance. "It's your fault for getting pregnant. I told you I didn't want a family."

And who would want a family with you? Maggie thought silently.

She felt sick, repulsed to the core of her being. To think she had found this man attractive, slept with him, and even considered a future with him…

"It's not too late, Kyle…" She hesitated. Kyle? She had to stop calling him that. That was his middle name. In real life, he was Ed—the school psychologist, a respectable man by day. Maggie closed her eyes. Was this even happening?

Edward didn't answer. He brushed the sweat from his forehead with his shirt sleeve. The car slowed as he took a right turn onto a better road—a narrow country lane of black asphalt. Maggie felt a glimmer of hope. Perhaps she might see a farmer's tractor or another car.

Edward accelerated, and the car shot dangerously down the narrow road. Maggie gritted her teeth and braced herself. The road curved, with hills to her right and open green farmland to her left. She knew that if another car appeared ahead, Edward wouldn't be able to brake in time.

"Stop!" she cried out.

He didn't listen. His crazed eyes were fixed on the road, the snarl now a permanent fixture on his face. She saw rage in those eyes, and fear consumed her.

He had taken her phone earlier. When he stopped the car, there was a brief struggle, and she had to surrender it. The doors were locked; she couldn't open them. She patted her pockets down. No pen—something she could have used as a weapon. But she did have a hairpin.

Pretending to fix her hair, she located the pin. She glanced at Edward. He was focused on the road. Maggie pulled the hairpin out and hid it in the palm of her hand. Carefully, she worked her thumb and forefinger to straighten it.

She scanned for road signs but saw none. These narrow lanes crisscrossed the North York Moors, diving between hills and valleys. She wasn't sure where they were, but she had a vague idea of their direction. If they followed this road, they could be heading north towards Whitby. Edward was avoiding the main dual carriageway to evade capture.

Without warning, he took a left turn, barely slowing down. The car skidded, dust covering the windscreen as Maggie was slammed against Edward. She screamed, and he pushed her away. The car straightened, the wipers working furiously.

Maggie steadied herself, panic tightening in her chest. She looked at her empty hands. She had dropped the hairpin. Frustration gnawed at her. She glanced at Edward again, then searched her lap and the sides of the seat. She couldn't make it obvious she was looking for something. She couldn't find the hairpin. Her heart sank.

The car began to slow. Up ahead, on the left, she saw a ramshackle building—a derelict barn. Its weather-beaten structure looked big, with the roof and walls intact but aged by decades of neglect. Wind and rain had chipped away at the thick stone walls.

Edward stopped the car and got out. Maggie unbuckled her seatbelt. Her door opened, and Edward stood there, watching her closely.

"Don't scream," he said.

He reached into his pocket and pulled out a small object. With a click, a long, wicked blade flicked out. Maggie gasped. Edward's cold, lifeless eyes stared at her.

"I'll kill you slowly, one cut at a time. It'll be nice to watch you suffer." He smiled, without mirth. "To think, you were one of the detectives on my trail. Well, you found me."

She stared at him in shock. He was enjoying this.

Edward reached out, grabbed the collar of her coat, and dragged her out of the car. Maggie wasn't weak; she could handle herself. But Edward was far stronger.

"Stand against the car and put your hands behind your back," he ordered.

He pressed the knife's sharp tip against her neck and dragged it slowly up to her chin, forcing her to lift it. Maggie shut her eyes.

"I'll slice this down your cheek and disfigure you permanently. Do you understand?"

Maggie nodded silently.

"Stand against the car and put your hands behind your back," he repeated.

She obeyed. She heard him put the knife away, but before she could move, she felt rope against her wrists. Expertly, Edward tied her hands together, then pushed her gently towards the barn.

Maggie stopped outside the closed door. Edward gripped the big brass handle with both hands and tugged four times before the heavy door creaked open.

They entered. The barn was dank and cold, as she had expected, but to her surprise, there was a light switch. Bright white overhead lights flickered on. Against the wall was a portable generator. At the rear, the space had been converted into a garage. A white van stood there, looking almost new.

Her heart sank. She realised Edward had a plan. She wasn't getting out of this easily. She had to think, to delay him somehow.

Edward pulled her inside and forced her to sit on a chair. He tied her ankles together with another piece of rope, then stood back.

"If you scream, I'll hear it." He took out the switchblade again. "You know what happens then."

He blindfolded her, tying it securely around her eyes. She couldn't see anything. Moments later, she heard him go outside. The car engine started, and the sound of tyres crunching stones faded into the distance.

Now, there was nothing but the wind whistling through the cracks.

Her ears strained. Then she heard footsteps, stopping close to her. He took off the blindfold and untied her legs. Then he pulled her to standing. He pushed her towards the white van.

Maggie stopped. "I need to pee. Please."

He stared at her coldly. "If you try anything…" He pulled out the knife again and held it against her cheek, the blade cold and hard against her skin. She swallowed, closed her eyes.

"Yes… I know."

He pulled her to the rear of the barn. Next to the white van, she saw a stack of number plates. There were also two large paint spray machines, and a blue residue on the ground. The van had changed colour, and probably plates as well.

She had bought herself a little time. But she had to think of a way to delay him further.

CHAPTER 3

"Where is Ed Warren's car?" Rita fumed.

"I can't see it, guv." Madeleine, the Traffic Sergeant, looked frantically between the bank of CCTV screens arranged on her desk.

"What about ANPR? He must have hit the main roads by now. Or any road with a passing police car, for heaven's sake."

"Not yet, guv. No alert on ANPR."

Rita turned to her detective sergeant, Richard Staveley, standing next to her. "Any news from Maggie's house?"

"Rizwan and a team of uniforms are searching the area around her house. Her mother hasn't heard from her. Her phone's switched off."

"Same as us then. Are the drones overhead?"

"They will be." Richard fished out his phone. "Not got a message from them yet. Shouldn't be long."

Rita shook her head, scanning the bank of CCTV monitors arrayed over Madeleine's desk. The sergeant got up from her chair, and Rita stepped back to let her pass. Then her eyes resumed scanning. She was looking at live images from cameras covering the main roads encircling North Ridings Forest, the North York Moors, and the routes around Scarborough. There were three main roads and a few smaller ones with cameras.

The problem was the tangle of country lanes snaking through the vast hills and valleys of the Moors. Her best hope of finding Ed Warren's car was via a drone or helicopter. One helicopter was already in the sky over Maggie's house in East Ayton, a village close to Hutton Buscel, where Ed Warren lived with his mother, Edna.

Ed Warren drove a black Audi, and they had the licence plates. But Rita feared he wasn't acting alone. He had planned this getaway in advance. Due to Matt's quick thinking, Ed hadn't escaped with him, but instead, he had taken Maggie. Now, he could switch vehicles or set up a decoy car for the police to chase—Ed had options.

He also had the advantage of time. Rita had only discovered Maggie's disappearance because her mother, Susan, had called the police when she couldn't get hold of her. It was now 5 p.m., and darkness was gathering at the edges of the horizon. As night shrouded the skies, it also dimmed Rita's hopes of finding Maggie before morning.

Susan's house had security cameras over the front door, capturing Edward Kyle Warren and Maggie Long getting into his black Audi. The same car Ed had driven to school and back every day—while Matt had languished in the basement of his farm. Rita shuddered at the thought. Even worse, Ed had now escaped with one of her own team members. She liked Maggie. She was a lovely person, hardworking and dynamic. A go-getter, just as Rita had been in her younger days. Rita clenched her jaw. There was no way she was letting go of Maggie. She would trawl the Moors herself if she had to.

Madeleine returned and resumed scanning the monitors. The Scarborough Traffic Control office was small. Besides Madeleine, three other officers were also searching for the black Audi.

Rita's phone rang. It was Rizwan. "Guv, I'm with Edna Warren. I asked if Edward had any other cars or friends in the area with cars. She didn't know, but she told me the Warren family owns four other farms in the area. They're scattered around the Moors, and there's one near Bempton Cliffs. That's where we traced Stuart to. Matt was kept there for a day."

"Yes, I remember. Where are the others?"

"I've got the village names here. I've sent squad cars to check them out. I'll stay here until they report back."

"Keep me posted," Rita said, then hung up. She looked out of the window of the fourth-floor office. Lights flickered on in the buildings opposite the police station.

She felt restless. She needed to be where Maggie might be held. She suspected Ed had stopped somewhere. The winding country lanes weren't easy to navigate in the dark. Alternatively, he might be trying to get as far away as possible. He would know the police would check the farms he had inherited. Rita didn't think he would go there.

She turned to Richard. "Have you got your car here?" He nodded.

"Let's go to Maggie's house and follow the road Ed took."

CHAPTER 4

Maggie watched as the twin beams of the white van's headlights illuminated the dark road. The van was travelling fast, taking corners at speed. Her hands were tied, as were her feet. She glanced at Ed. His face was bathed in the eerie green glow from the dashboard.

"Ed. Please stop this. We need to go back."

Her words fell on deaf ears. He ignored her, his manic eyes fixed on the thin strip of asphalt ahead.

Maggie heard a roaring sound above, and seconds later, a helicopter appeared overhead. Ed cut the headlights immediately and slowed down. The narrow lane had no place to pull over. After the helicopter roared past, he kept the lights off but started moving again, slower this time.

Maggie had already tried the doors, but they were locked. So were the windows. With a sinking heart, she watched as the helicopter swept past them. It switched on a searchlight, its beam piercing the darkness, but it moved away. Maggie felt like screaming at it, telling it to turn back. Ed seemed to sense her disquiet.

"Try anything funny," he said quietly, "and I'll put you to sleep and chuck you in the back."

Maggie gritted her teeth. "Why haven't you done that already?"

He didn't reply. His eyes remained fixed on the dwindling shape of the helicopter. The sound of its rotor blades faded into the distance.

Ed increased his speed. After a while, he flicked the headlights back on. Maggie knew they were heading deeper into the Moors, but she had no idea which direction they were travelling. The sight of the helicopter had given her hope. The police were searching for her. She knew the drones would be useless in the dark. They had searchlights too, but they weren't powerful.

Hope was slipping away. She looked out at the blackness of the hills, desperately wishing for even the smallest glimmer of light. Only the inky dark stared back at her. She had to do something.

"My belly's hurting from the seatbelt. I need to take it off."

Ed slowed the car and glanced at her. "I'm watching you."

Maggie couldn't manoeuvre her tied hands to the buckle, so Ed had to do it for her. She leaned against the car door and sighed in mock relief. Her feet were still bound, but she had slid sideways, giving her some leverage. She glanced at Ed. He was watching her, but most of his attention was on the narrow, winding road ahead.

Maggie flexed her toes, then her ankles. The rope chafed against her skin. But she had long legs, and she could still use them.

In one fluid motion, she slid lower in her seat, lifting her legs up until she was almost lying down, knees bent. Then, with all the force she could muster, she drove her heavy boots into Ed's shoulder, slamming him against the door.

Ed swore, trying to fend her off with one hand while keeping control of the van with the other. But her legs were stronger. He lost control. The van veered off to the right, skidding across the road before crashing into a stone wall.

***

"Oscar Tango to Sierra Foxtrot, do you receive?" The voice crackled through Rita's radio. She turned the black dial and pressed the button.

"Receiving, Oscar Tango. Do you have a visual?"

The helicopter pilot's voice faded into static before returning. Rita could hear the rotor blades spinning in the background, a dull, muffled thrum through his noise-cancelling headset.

"Not yet, but we passed a van twenty-two miles northwest of Sawdon village. We saw the headlights briefly, then they vanished. Could have taken a turning or switched them off. I did a sweep but saw nothing. Just letting you know."

Rita turned to Richard, who was listening. "Did you get that?"

"Yes. We've just passed Sawdon, as it happens. Get the coordinates, and I'll put them into the satnav."

Rita relayed the message, and within seconds, they had the location.

"Oscar Tango," she spoke into the radio, "have you seen any other vehicles?"

"Not yet."

"Circle back to where you saw the van. We'll rendezvous with you on location."

"Copy that, Sierra Foxtrot."

Richard pressed down on the accelerator, and Rita grabbed the overhead handle, bracing herself.

"Hope you did your obstacle course this year," she muttered.

"Not yet, guv," Richard replied.

The night sky blurred past the window. Rita was flung sideways, then pressed against the door as Richard took a high-speed turn. With a screech of tyres, the car straightened. A few minutes later, Rita's heart leapt into her throat. Their headlights caught a white van. It had crashed into the stone fence bordering the lane.

A man was standing by the passenger door, pulling someone out. He froze when he heard the approaching car, headlights blazing.

"Ed Warren!" Rita shouted.

Richard slammed on the brakes, and Rita jumped out, torch in one hand, baton in the other. She sprinted towards the van, flicking the baton to its full length.

Ed had left Maggie on the road, and she was slumped against the vehicle. Rita dropped to her knees beside her.

"I'm okay," Maggie gasped. "Go get him."

Richard was already in pursuit. Ed had vaulted the stone wall and was sprinting up the hill. Rita thrust her radio into Maggie's hands.

"Call for backup. The bird should be here soon." She pointed skywards, and Maggie understood.

Rita turned and scrambled over the stone fence. She perched on the top, swung her legs over, and dropped down the other side. Her ankles jarred, but she kept her balance.

Her torch beam picked out Richard, closing the gap on a shadowy figure ahead. Rita pushed herself harder, lungs burning with the effort. She saw Richard leap, tackling Ed to the ground.

"He might be armed!" Rita shouted.

Richard grunted as he wrestled Ed. Then suddenly, he fell backwards. Ed had grabbed a rock and hurled it at Rita. She ducked, and the stone sailed over her head.

Ed turned to run, but Rita was faster. She launched herself into a sliding tackle that would have made a footballer proud. Her outstretched leg clipped Ed's ankles, sending him sprawling.

Before he could recover, Rita was on him. She straddled his back, forcing him down as Richard caught up. He grabbed Ed's hands and delivered a sharp punch to the back of his head.

Rita yanked the handcuffs from her belt, and together, they snapped them onto Ed's wrists.

The helicopter's roar grew deafening. A gust of wind blasted down as it hovered overhead, its spotlight slicing through the darkness, turning night into day.

"Edward Kyle Warren," Rita shouted over the noise. "You're under arrest."

CHAPTER 5

Susan had joined them, and the three of them sat there chatting. Rita could tell Susan couldn't wait to be a grandmother. She was trying to be serious given the situation, but her excitement was apparent in the gleam in her eyes. She confessed she had already started looking at baby clothes.

Rita laughed but also felt a little sad. She had never had a mother; she would never share this special bond. Bittersweet memories played in her mind as she watched the dust motes dancing in the sun's rays.

Her radio buzzed, breaking into her thoughts.

"Deceased female found on South Beach, Scarborough. CID, please respond."

Rita frowned, and Maggie looked at her with concern. Rita picked up her radio and stepped outside onto the landing.

She spoke into her radio. "DI Gupta from CID. What happened?"

"Morning, guv. Darren Broadbent from Uniform speaking. It was reported last night, actually. A couple found the woman on South Beach. She was in a rocky cove, partly covered with sand. Uniforms have secured the scene. SOCO is informed and en route."

"Thanks. Send me the location, please, and I'll see you there. Any sign of the media?"

She could hear the smile in Darren's voice. He was a veteran inspector of the NYP. "Not yet, but it won't be long."

"Aye. See you soon."

The waves lapped softly against the shore as the pale morning sun struggled to break through a blanket of low-hanging clouds. Rita wrapped her coat tightly around her against the chill of Scarborough's South Beach. The wind carried the salt tang of the sea, mingled with the dampness of the sand beneath her boots.

Ahead, a stretch of blue and white crime scene tape fluttered in the breeze, cordoning off a small area near the tideline. Beyond it, a craggy rock formation loomed. Rita could see a white forensic tent being erected. A path at the end of the promenade led down to the beach. A white Scene of Crime van stood on the sloping path.

Rita made her way across the sand, stepping carefully onto the sterile boards placed at regular intervals. She glanced up at the promenade. A few inquisitive visitors had already gathered. It wouldn't be long before the local press got wind of it.

She approached the rock formation—an impressive sight. Two huge boulders faced the sea, resting on a collection of smaller rocks. They formed a kind of temple, Rita thought. The inner circle, where the white tent was being erected, was secluded from the wind and rain.

Shola Adebayo, the lead Scenes of Crime Officer, stood nearby, clipboard in hand, wearing a pair of blue overalls already dusted with sand. She looked up as Rita approached.

"Morning, DI Gupta," Shola said, her tone light. The dancing light in her eyes told Rita she was using Rita's official title in jest. They had become friends over the past year. Her expression softened as she touched Rita's arm with a gloved hand.

"Heard about Maggie. Poor lass. Is she all right?"

"As well as can be expected," Rita sighed. "She's traumatised but should make a full recovery." She didn't elaborate. No one needed to know about Maggie's delicate situation. Not right now, anyway. She indicated the body, getting back to business.

"Unpleasant one for a beach stroll, isn't it?"

"Not nice at all. But good morning to you just the same."

"Oh, aye." Shola grinned. "Wish I could be the bearer of better news."

"Such is our lot," Rita sighed. "What have we got?"

"Female, twenties, IC3. South Asian, judging by her features. No ID, no phone, no bag. Just her." Shola gestured toward the body. "Hands folded over her chest, legs flat. Partially buried by the sand, as you can see, up to waist level."

Rita crouched down at the edge of the scene, careful not to disturb anything. There was no sign of blood on the sand or any struggle. The sand had been carefully scooped up around the body, covering her up to the waist. The woman's eyes were wide and staring, as if she couldn't believe what had happened to her. Her skin was pale brown, the purple splashes of livor mortis beginning to appear. It would be easier to spot on Caucasian skin, but regardless, Rita didn't think this woman had been dead long. Livor mortis became fixed about six to twelve hours after death.

Her long black hair fanned out around her head, matted with wet sand. Her neatly folded hands gave the strange impression that she'd been laid to rest.

A blue synthetic blouse clung to her upper body, covered by a red coat. The clothes looked cheap and had seen better days. The woman's vacant eyes stared at the sky. Rita moved closer, taking care not to disturb the white circles SOCO officers had marked on the sand. One of them was kneeling, taking a swab sample of some fluids they had spotted.

As Rita got closer, she noticed bruising on the woman's neck—possible signs of strangulation.

"No obvious wounds?" Rita asked.

"Apart from the neck, none that we can see at the moment," Shola replied. "Dr Das might have more insight."

"Whoever put her here knew about the tide lines, didn't they? The body wasn't washed out to sea," Rita observed.

Shola nodded. "I thought about that. The tide doesn't come all the way up here. There's a natural dip in the sand. The bank breaks about there." She pointed towards the sea with her pen. Rita followed her direction and saw the gentle downslope in the sandy beach.

Did someone with local knowledge do this? But the tide tables were published daily in local papers and online. Anyone could know them with a little effort. Bathers and strollers certainly did.

Rita had her gloves on as she gently pressed the torso. It didn't have the rubbery stiffness of rigor mortis. The legs, still covered in sand, would have been more telling. The chest, abdomen, and legs held the largest muscles of the body, and it took about twelve hours for rigor to fully set in. But the abdominal muscles were still fairly lax. From her rudimentary knowledge of pathology, Rita estimated the woman hadn't been dead for longer than twelve hours.

On the hands, she noted signs of struggle—scrapes on the knuckles and a couple of loose nails. This woman had fought for her life. The killer had left a mark, and that would be useful. Rita crouched and slid the cardigan down from the woman's wrist. A yellow bangle appeared, encrusted with small stones. Whether they were precious, she couldn't tell. The design was granular, rough to the touch. Gold, she thought.

A faint memory stirred, like seaweed ruffled by the wind. Clara, her mother, had golden bangles just like this—gifts from her father, Jay, who was of Indian origin. This bangle looked so similar.

Footsteps approached from the direction of the promenade. Richard Staveley, her detective sergeant, arrived at her side. Short and podgy, his coat strained against his pot belly. His blond hair was windblown, his coat flecked with sea spray.

"All right, guv. Got here as soon as I could. What do you think?" Richard asked, scanning the scene.

"Too early to say," Rita replied. "But whoever left her here went to some effort. The hands, the sand… almost as if it's her grave."

She shivered. A ritual killing suggested premeditation. A sick exhibition, she thought. She hadn't expected this in a quiet town like Scarborough.

Richard crouched down. "No shoe prints." He looked at the access road. "Checked?"

"No boot prints," Shola said. "But signs of disturbed sand."

Rita pursed her lips. Looking up at the promenade, she noted the lack of CCTV cameras nearby. This had been planned meticulously.

Was the victim brought here or killed here?

Henry, crouched at the victim's feet, uncovered white trainers. Worn, scuffed.

"Brand name," he murmured. "Paragon."

Rita frowned. A cheap brand. South Asian features. The bangle.

Was this woman new to these shores?

CHAPTER 6

Dr Das arrived, his black medical briefcase in hand. A slim, tall, bespectacled man in a blue coat to ward off the wind, he stepped carefully across the sand toward the body. Rita gave him a brief nod as he crouched beside the young woman.

"Hello, Doc."

"Hi, Rita." He shook his head at the scene. "Not an ideal way to start the morning. When was it reported?"

"Late last night. Uniforms protected the scene, and we were informed this morning. A couple found the body. I haven't spoken to them yet."

Dr Das pulled on a pair of gloves and crouched by the woman's body. He placed his briefcase on the piece of tarpaulin stretched around the corpse. Taking out his rectal thermometer, he gestured for Shola and Rita to help undress the victim and turn her onto her left side. Dr Das took the reading and grimaced.

"Her core temperature is about seven degrees lower than ambient. That suggests she's been dead for approximately six to eight hours. I would place the time of death between midnight and 2 a.m. I'll have a more precise estimate once I input the numbers into my spreadsheet."

He stood up stiffly, his knees popping, and moved carefully towards the victim's head.

"Eyes are open," he observed. "Which suggests definite rigor mortis here, keeping the eye muscles flexed, hence open."

"Earrings in place," he murmured. Rita had noticed them too. Stud earrings, gold, with some inlaid stones—matching the bangles. She mentioned them, and Dr Das glanced at the left wrist, nodding.

Rita said, "Leaving the jewellery was deliberate. He went through all the trouble of laying her out like this because he wanted her preserved. His own macabre show."

Dr Das looked up, his dark eyes meeting Rita's. He spoke softly. "A malignant narcissistic personality. They want their work displayed to the world."

"And men like him strike again," Rita said. The wind scattered across the sand, whistling against the rocks. She shivered. Most serial killers had what psychiatrists termed malignant narcissistic personality disorder.

"But let's not jump to conclusions," she added. "One swallow doesn't make a summer. We need to check our databases for similar victims."

"Indeed," Dr Das said. He pointed at the neck. "Bruise marks on the neck and tracheal deviation. That suggests strangulation and a ruptured trachea. Have you seen the subconjunctival haemorrhages?"

Rita hadn't, so she moved closer with Richard and Shola. Dr Das pointed at the jagged black marks on the whites of the woman's eyes.

"Ah yes," Rita said. "The blood vessels burst due to pressure applied to the neck, right? That causes elevated pressure in the eyeballs."

"Yes," Dr Das smiled, looking impressed. "Hence these marks—blood turns black when it leaks out of the capillaries, or tiny blood vessels on the surface of the sclera, as the whites of the eyes are called."

The veteran pathologist's practiced eye swept over the remainder of the body.

"No ligature marks on her wrists or ankles," Dr Das noted, gently lifting one of the folded hands. "But she does have knuckle lacerations and sand embedded under her nails, which indicate she struggled—perhaps clawed at the ground."

"Or at her killer. There might be skin cells," Rita murmured. "We'll need a DNA analysis from those samples."

Dr Das looked rueful, shaking his head. "Her hands being folded like this—it's like a ritual."

"Have you seen this before, around here?" Rita asked. "I've seen serial killers advertise their work, but I haven't come across this particular MO."

"No," Dr Das said. "This is new to me. Frankly, I never thought I'd see anything like this in a small seaside town like Scarborough."

Henry approached Shola, holding a see-through plastic evidence bag. Inside was a golden chain necklace with a small pendant.

"I found them separately," Henry said. "Looks like they were ripped from her neck. Maybe her attacker didn't find them in the sand."

Shola held up the bag, studying the broken necklace. "Simple, cheap. No markings or identifiers. Could be personal. But the pendant is..."

Rita stepped closer and examined it. "That's an elephant head shape." She frowned. "That looks like an Indian design. The women in my dad's family wear stuff like that."

"It might help us figure out who she is," she said, showing the pendant to Dr Das. He squinted at it, adjusting his glasses.

"That definitely looks ethnic. Indian, I'd say. This wasn't on the victim, was it?"

"No. Henry just found it."

"And not far away," Henry added. He pointed to a spot about ten yards closer to the sea. "The sand is more disturbed there as well, and there are some partial shoe prints. I think the victim and killer got into a fight there."

Rita went over to have a look. Henry was right. She felt a surge of excitement as she examined the faint smudges of shoes. This could be valuable for the forensic boot match database.

"Is Bob Chandler coming later?" Rita asked. Richard answered.

"He's aware of the scene, aye. He should be here this afternoon."

As the SOCOs and Dr Das continued their work, Rita stepped back to survey the scene. The tide crept closer, threatening to erase what little evidence remained.

Rita thought of the woman—young, with a life ahead of her until someone took it away. Who was she? What had brought her to this lonely stretch of beach in the dead of night? Was she local, or had she been brought here?

She'd been left here to be found, but by whom? And why?

"Guv." Richard's voice pulled her from her thoughts. He stood at the edge of the scene, motioning toward the access road. "You might want to see this."

Rita followed him to the path, where Shola's team had cast the faint tyre tracks. The grooves were uneven, suggesting a heavy load. Sand clung to the treads. A van, perhaps? It wasn't much, but it was something.

"All right," Rita said. "Get casts of these and inform Bob. He might be able to get a match. Check CCTV from nearby roads. If a vehicle was here last night, I want to know where it came from and where it went."

Richard nodded. "The driver would know they got caught on CCTV. Would the killer really take that risk?"

Rita shook her head. "Too early to say. He might've wanted to keep an eye on the scene. These sick bastards can be like that."

As the wind picked up, Rita turned her back to the sea. The killer hadn't been as thorough as he thought. Or had he?

It was clear he wanted to make a statement, and play cat and mouse with the police. Like Richard, Rita scanned the road above. A few cars passed by. Pedestrians were walking past, and they were still few, but cast inquisitive looks at the scene below. She was glad the SOC technicians were now erecting the white forensic tent, and it was almost complete.

Any minute now, she expected the media to arrive. Scarborough was a quiet town apart from the summer tourist season, but an event like this would be big news.

Dr Das approached her. "I'll be heading back to the hospital. The post mortem should be ready tomorrow morning. Hope that's okay?"

"That's fine, thank you."

Dr Das's calm eyes studied her. Rita felt comfortable in the older man's presence. He had a relaxed manner, and she had come to realise he was a discreet man, who kept his affairs to himself. She trusted him.

"You need to get a positive ID. I guess it all flows from there." He smiled. "I think our victim is in your capable hands." The smile faded from his face as he realised the portent of his words.

"She is," Rita said. "And I won't let her down."

CHAPTER 7

The elegant Victorian façade of the Grand Scarborough Hotel loomed over the seafront, its weathered exterior bathed in the soft, overcast light of the morning. Rita and Richard walked up the wide stone steps, their footsteps echoing in the quiet entrance hall.

The receptionist, a young woman with tired eyes, directed them to a room on the third floor where the witnesses were waiting.

The knock on the door was answered almost immediately. A man in his late twenties, pale and visibly shaken, stood in the doorway. He wore a crumpled sweatshirt and tracksuit bottoms, his hair dishevelled as though he hadn't slept.

"Mr Haywood?" Rita asked gently, flashing her warrant card. "I'm Detective Inspector Rita Gupta, and this is Sergeant Richard Staveley."

"Yes," he replied, his voice hoarse. "We were expecting you. Come in."

Inside, the hotel room was modest but comfortable. A woman, also in her late twenties, sat on the edge of the bed, clutching a steaming mug of tea with both hands. She looked up as the detectives entered, her face a picture of exhaustion and distress.

"Thank you for speaking with us," Rita said. "I know this must be difficult for you both."

The man nodded, pulling a chair from the small table by the window and sitting down. "I'm Ethan Haywood, and this is my partner, Rachel. We're here on holiday. Well, we were supposed to be."

Rachel gave a weak nod, her gaze fixed on her mug. "It doesn't feel much like a holiday anymore." She looked up at Rita. "To be honest, we just want to get out of here now. Can we, please?"

"Once you've spoken to us, and we've confirmed we don't need to see you again, then yes, you can."

Rachel frowned, anxiety rippling across her face. "What do you mean?"

Rita felt sorry for the woman. She had to keep an open mind about the suspects, but she didn't think Rachel was lying or being deceptive. She didn't look like she was capable of killing the woman on the beach.

"We just need to speak to you, that's all." Rita smiled, trying to put her mind at ease. Rachel looked at Ethan uncertainly.

"Can you tell us what happened last night?" Rita began, her pen poised over her black notebook.

Ethan glanced at Rachel before speaking. "We'd been out for dinner. Nothing fancy, just a place along the promenade. Then we hit one of the DJ bars in town. It was past midnight when we finished. On the way back, we decided to stop by the beach… you know, to do something spontaneous. We thought we'd go for a swim."

Rachel's cheeks flushed, but she didn't lift her gaze. "It was silly, I know. We were drunk. The beach was empty, and it felt like… like we could do something a bit wild. So we stripped off and ran into the water."

"What time was this?"

Ethan said, "Around half past midnight."

"Did you notice anything unusual when you got there?" Rita asked.

Ethan shook his head. "No, not at first. It was quiet. Really quiet. We left our clothes near the rock formation and went in. But then…" He paused, swallowing hard. "When we came back out and got dressed, that's when I literally stumbled over her."

Rachel's hands tightened around the mug, her knuckles whitening. "I thought it was an animal or something. You know, a fox, maybe. I don't know," she whispered. "But then Ethan went closer, and… God, she was just lying there."

"What did you do next?" Rita asked, her voice soft.

Ethan ran a hand through his hair. "I told Rachel to grab her clothes and get dressed. Then I called the police. I didn't touch her, didn't go too close. I didn't know what to do. She wasn't moving. We knew she was dead."

"Did you see anyone else on the beach? Any vehicles or unusual activity?"

Both of them shook their heads.

"No," Ethan said. "It was just us. But we weren't there for long before we saw her. Whoever left her there… they must have been gone already."

Richard spoke up. "Think carefully. Did you see or hear anything? On the promenade? Or on the road?"

Ethan frowned. "There was one thing. While I was calling the police, I noticed the lights of a car. It was just sitting on the road, by the promenade. The lights came on, and it moved past slowly. I couldn't help thinking someone was watching us."

Rita and Richard exchanged a glance. Richard said, "You didn't mention this before."

"No, but speaking to you now, it's coming back to me. It was odd, how slowly the car moved past. For a while, the headlights pointed directly at us, then the car moved."

Rita knew this was an important breakthrough. That car would be caught on CCTV, and potentially, they could identify the driver.

"Do you remember what sort of car it was?"

"It was a van. Blue. It was lit up under the streetlamps, that's how I remember. And there was no other car on the road. It seemed odd."

"You didn't get the registration number, by any chance?"

"No, sorry."

"Did you see the driver?"

Ethan thought for a while, his brows furrowing. "It was hard to tell. I can't be sure. There was one person in the driver's seat. A man, I think."

Rita glanced at Rachel. "How about you?"

"I didn't see it. I mean, I was just…"

Ethan spoke for her. "I was holding Rachel. She had her back to the road. I was facing the road, with my back to the sea."

"And you didn't see the van there when you went down to the beach?"

Ethan paused. He frowned, thinking hard. Then he shook his head. "I'm sorry. We were tipsy. I wasn't paying much attention."

Rita's mind was racing. Serial killers liked to see their macabre actions get attention. They wanted to know people had noticed their evil handiwork. She had to find that van and its driver, without delay.

"Thank you. Please stay in Scarborough till the end of today. Then you should be free to go."

CHAPTER 8

The Scarborough Police Station front desk and reception had its usual smattering of drunks from the night before. A few people sat in the green plastic seats, waiting anxiously for news of their loved ones—the families of those the police had no choice but to bring in.

Rita and Richard walked past them and through the double doors at the back, which slid open when Richard pressed his ID card against the digital reader on the wall. The open-plan office was alive with its usual rhythm: ringing phones, the hum of printers, and the occasional burst of laughter cutting through the background noise. Uniformed officers shared the space with detectives.

They passed through and turned left into the CID Branch office, where Detective Constable Rizwan Ahmed was hunched over a computer, tapping away. He looked up as they approached, his face breaking into a grin.

"Now then, our dynamic duo," Rizwan said, leaning back in his chair. "All good at the crime scene?"

"Yes, we've been working away while you're wasting time here," Richard said.

Rizwan looked hurt. "Not fair. I've been scouring the databases for similar MOs and checking missing persons."

Rita had already updated Rizwan about the victim's appearance and ethnic origin.

"And did you find owt?" Richard asked, dropping into the chair beside him. "Or are you still checking out films on that streaming app?"

"Speaking of streaming, your very capable DC—me—has been liaising with Traffic, and we've got footage of a van. It's blue and looks old, which matches what the skinny-dipper mentioned. Trouble is, it disappears after that. Doesn't show up on any other cameras nearby."

"You have been very capable," Rita said, shifting closer to Rizwan's desk to look at his screen. "What time was this?"

"About one a.m." Rizwan brought up the footage. Parked opposite a streetlamp, the blue van's colour was just about visible. The driver wasn't. The hulking form of the Grand Hotel loomed a few yards up the road. Apart from sporadic pools of light puncturing the darkness, everything else was shrouded in shadow.

"We've got the registration. I filled out the V888 form with the DVLA and am waiting for the list of registered owners."

"Good work. Let's see if we can get the driver's details. Did ANPR not pick up the van again?"

Automatic Number Plate Recognition was used across the UK to track vehicles.

"Not so far."

Richard rubbed his chin. "Hmm. That makes me wonder if he used fake plates or if he stopped and swapped them."

"Even if he changed the plates, we should still be able to see the van. He can't change the colour, can he? And how could he always be in CCTV dark spots?" Rita frowned. "Scarborough and North Yorkshire don't have as many cameras as a city, but still."

Had the killer scoped out the cameras beforehand? If so, why let the van be seen? He could've parked anywhere else. Maybe he had no choice. Perhaps he wanted to see the body once before driving off, and this was the best vantage point.

"How long was he at that spot?" Rita asked.

Rizwan played the footage again. "Only five minutes. He drove off quickly."

Rita watched the red tail lights vanish into the night. No other car appeared on the desolate stretch of road. Morning was different, she knew. That road was busy with pedestrians and workers heading into town.

"Keep at it," Rita said. "Anything else?"

"There's the golden bangle and the necklace with the elephant pendant. I uploaded the photos online for a match, but there's loads of Indian jewellery like that. You can buy it here too. My mum knows people who wear that stuff."

Rita thought about the woman's clothes and shoes. "What about the shoe brand, Paragon? Have you checked?"

"Not yet." Rizwan did a quick search. "Ah, yes. That's a popular brand in India."

"Why would she be wearing thin Indian shoes on a cold night in Scarborough? And on the sand?" Richard raised his hands. "She might be a tourist, but even a tourist wouldn't do that."

"Maybe they were the only shoes she had?" Rita suggested. "Like the cheap clothes she wore?"

"She was thin," Richard said quietly. "I saw how slender her arms were." He didn't say more, but Rita understood. She agreed. Perhaps the victim had fallen on hard times. Maybe she was homeless.

"Anything on missing persons?" Rita asked Rizwan.

"Nowt yet, guv. Nothing matching her description. I checked the national database."

Rita leaned against the wall. The cement felt cold on her back. "There are South Asian community centres in Scarborough, right? Let's ask there."

"I know where they are," Rizwan said. "And if there are any more, my mum will know. I can ring the council too. There must be an Indian community centre somewhere."

"Look for temples and mosques online," Rita instructed. "And community centres. South Asian shops are good too—they're big, and the local community visits daily. Let's make an e-fit and distribute it. Put up posters around town. Yes, that will alert the media, but we need to make a positive ID ASAP."

Rizwan nodded. "On it, guv."

Richard stood. "I'll have a chat with the Audio-Visual team about the e-fit."

As the team got to work, Rita's desk phone buzzed. She picked it up, her stomach sinking at the clipped voice on the other end.

"DI Gupta. My office. Now."

Detective Superintendent Nicola Perkins didn't wait for a reply before hanging up. Rita exhaled sharply and glanced at Richard and Rizwan. "That was the D Sup. Wish me luck."

"Rather you than me," Richard muttered. "Don't let her wind you up."

Detective Superintendent Nicola Perkins's office was pristine. Her desk looked as if a robot had arranged everything: coloured pens on one side, black and blue pens opposite. Two sheets of white paper in the middle. A closed black laptop to her right. The name badge, stating her position, faced upwards as if to remind visitors who was in charge.

The small woman sat with her arms folded, her button-like nose and lips pinched, looking as if she'd got out of the wrong side of the bed. The oversized chair made her seem even smaller. Her blonde hair was pulled into a severe ponytail, and her sharp cheekbones and chin jutted upwards.

Rita didn't know what Nicola had against her. She had fought ambitious men all her life in the force and was used to combative superiors. But she had never encountered a female boss like Nicola. Even after a year in Scarborough, the woman still treated her like an unwanted junior detective begging for a job.

Power struggle? Something else? Rita didn't care. She just wanted to do her job—for herself and her team.

"Superintendent Perkins," she said, nodding.

Nicola didn't move, only her lips. "The duty uniforms team are in a dizzy. The media will have a field day. South Beach, of all places, to find a young woman's body. Do we have an ID?"

Her tone was accusatory, as if the murder were Rita's fault.

Rita stiffened, and cut her eyes at Nicola, and she thought she saw the woman's lips twitch.

"Even miracles take longer than a couple of hours. Ma'am." Rita spoke slowly, keeping her eyes on Nicola. She wasn't afraid of her boss. Rita could quit right now, and go back to her old job in London. It wouldn't be easy, but she had that option. Nicola, would be left in a hole, scrambling to find a senior DI to fill Rita's shoes. The high voltage glare that Nicola directed at Rita could've melted steel. Rita met her eyes full on. For the life of her she couldn't imagine what Nicola had against her. But some people were just like that. But Rita was used to not giving an inch to people like Nicola.

Nicola spoke through clenched lips. "It would be a miracle if this didn't blow up in our faces, and cause national headlines. We need a resolution quickly. Has the body been removed from the beach?"

"Yes, ma'am."

"I want a report on my desk first thing tomorrow morning, so I can tell the Chief Constable we're making progress. Is that understood?"

"Crystal, ma'am."

"That will be all."

Rita turned and left the room. After she shut the door, she let out a pent-up breath. Then she smoothed down her jacket, and hurried down the corridor.

CHAPTER 9

Rita picked up three coffees from the canteen and bumped into Jack Banford as she walked down the corridor.

"I heard," Jack said. "Just spoke to Mark Botley. I was dealing with a case he was involved in last night."

Mark was one of the uniformed inspectors. Then again, Jack had a way of finding things out. He looked as handsome as ever in his sharply cut black suit and white shirt. The clothes fitted his athletic figure nicely. His melting brown eyes focused on her as he came closer. She could smell his aftershave; it was woody, dense, and pleasant.

"Get around, don't you?" Rita raised an eyebrow.

"Only with people who like me," Jack grinned. His smile faded. "This is going to be a big case. Nothing like this has happened here for ages. In fact, I can't remember a murder on the beach in all my years here."

Rita moved the coffee cups from one hand to the other. "The woman's South Asian. Not a big population here, is there?"

Jack shook his head. "No. But there is in Leeds and Bradford. They tend to live and work there. South Asians would have restaurant businesses, I guess."

He lowered his head, cutting Rita off. He seemed deep in thought. Then he looked at her, his eyebrows drawn together.

"Actually, one of our partners dealt with a case last year where a restaurant owner was trying to open a branch in Scarborough. His Indian restaurant chain was based in Leeds. The council wouldn't allow him to have the land because it was designated for residential development only. Not sure if that helps you, but the restaurant did get built, and I can check if it's still open."

"Thanks, Jack. We don't have an ID, so anything is useful, to be honest."

"Good," Jack said. "How's Maggie?"

"She's bearing up as best she can." Rita hesitated. Now wasn't the time to talk about Maggie, she felt. Jack saw it and took the words out of her mouth. Not words, but an idea she didn't want to put into words. Not aloud, anyway."What are you doing this evening?Jack was a childhood friend, one who had done well for himself in this area. As to what was happening between her and Jack, Rita honestly didn't know. They were good friends now. Many moons ago, Jack had been her first boyfriend. Well, she wasn't a pimple-faced teenager anymore, even if Jack still sometimes made her heart flutter. But she wasn't up for a flutter, or anything, right now. And yet… she felt something. She didn't want to admit it, but it was there.

"Not sure yet," she said honestly. "We might be working late tonight. We're a man down with Maggie off. Shall I call you?"

"Sure. I'll finish around seven."

Jack walked Rita back to the office and opened the door for her. She waved goodbye to him, put the coffees on the table, and handed them out to the men, who were on the phone.

Rita opened up her laptop to see she had several emails from the uniformed team. They had been asking around town and putting up posters about the victim. She checked the missing persons database as well but didn't find anything of interest in the region. Two girls were reported missing in Leeds and York, but neither of them matched the victim's description.

Rizwan put the phone down and got her attention. "I just spoke to a woman who's the manager of a community centre for South Asian women in town. She recognised the elephant pendant and the white trainers. Shall we meet her with the e-fit photo?"

"Good idea. Anything else?"

Richard had hung up as well and was listening to them. "I called a few of the restaurants, but they're all shut now. I'll send uniforms later this afternoon or evening."

"I might have the details of a big restaurant soon," Rita said, recalling her conversation with Jack. "But yes, we need to focus on them. How many Indian restaurants in town?"

"Well," Rizwan said, "most of them are actually Bangladeshi. But regardless, they could still employ our victim, even though I think our victim is Indian, given her attire and jewellery."

"There are Indian restaurants in town," Richard said. Then he grinned. "I make a point to eat in a proper Indian, if I say so myself. There's one called the Tamarind near town, and my mate knows the owner. I got the owner's number. He's not answering, but I'll try him again."

"Aren't you an authentic Yorkshireman?" Rizwan grinned. "Only the best for you, eh?"

"It was less greasy and more vegetarian," Richard said. "Pretty good nosh, really."

"Must check out the Tamarind," Rizwan said.

"Not for dinner tonight," Rita said. "We've got work to do. Come on, let's get going."

The Roshni Community Centre was off Westgate Street, not far from Scarborough train station. Inside, the office space was open-plan, with a reception desk at the front. Two women sat there, looking at Rita and Rizwan inquisitively. Rita showed her warrant card to the women, and they inspected it closely. One was older, with white streaks in her hair, and the other appeared to be in her forties, Rita thought. Both were plump and dressed in traditional Indian salwar kameez.

"My name's Poonam Desai," the younger woman said. "I'm one of the coordinators here. I was expecting you. This is my colleague, Sheila."

Rita nodded in greeting, and Rizwan spoke from beside her. "I spoke to you, Poonam."

Poonam came out from behind the desk and led them down the open-plan office. Rita saw posters on the walls advising women of their rights in divorce or social conflict situations. The posters were in English as well as South Asian languages. She also noticed Polish among the languages. The workers were mostly female, a mixture of white and brown-skinned people. Several of them looked up, and one by one, they looked away when they met Rita's gaze.

As Rita walked into the office Poonam guided them to, she reflected on how different Scarborough was from when she had lived here. In her teenage years, she was one of the few children of colour in her class. She had been lucky to have good friends. Now, Scarborough was a changed town, with a more mixed population.

The office was small, with a green carpet and bookshelves crammed with journals and legal tomes. Rita and Rizwan sat down opposite Poonam. Rizwan showed her the e-fit photo, along with images of the jewellery and the victim's shoes.

Poonam studied them, then lifted her troubled eyes to them. "Yes, I remember her. I was out getting some breakfast just now when I saw the photo at the bus station. And when you called, that drove it home. She had that pendant. And those white shoes."

"What was her name?"

"Anika Joshi. We made an account for her, as she wanted to learn English and also wanted help to get a job."

"How did she get here? Did she have any family locally?"

"No, she was alone. She said she had recently moved from Bombay."

Rita studied Poonam. "From your experience, what would a single woman from India, without any family, be doing here?"

Poonam understood the tone in Rita's voice. "I don't know, Inspector," she said softly. "But she was guarded and didn't give too much away. She only wanted to find a job."

Rizwan scribbled a note in his pad. "Did she have an accent? Anything that might tell us where she was from?"

Poonam thought for a moment. "Her Hindi was fluent, and she spoke English okay."

"Did you speak to her in Hindi?" Rita asked.

"Yes." Poonam's eyes swept over Rita's face, and she knew what the woman was thinking. Rita had her mother's green eyes, but her skin was darker, taking after her father, Jayesh. Poonam had no doubt recognised Rita's mixed-race features.

"Did Anika say where she was staying?" Rita asked.

"Well, she entered an address when she opened the account with us, which is just us taking some details down in case employers ask for them."

"We would like to see that address. Did she have a phone?"

Poonam shook her head slowly. Rita got the distinct impression Poonam wasn't voicing the doubts in her mind.

"Did she have the right to work here?"

"Inspector, our employers don't do background checks. We have connections with the local factories, warehouses, and also smaller businesses like beauty salons and restaurants. They often employ migrants. They don't ask for work permits or visas."

"But a right to work is granted to foreigners who are here on certain types of visas," Rita said. "Are you saying the employers you know employ these people illegally?"

Poonam was looking flustered now. "No, it's not illegal. And of course, they need to have the right to work. Anika said she was a student and that she could work after her college hours, according to her student visa."

"A college in Scarborough?" Rizwan frowned. "For an overseas student?"

Poonam cleared her throat. "At the Scarborough Further Education College. She was doing the hair and beauty salon course."

"I didn't realise that course was open to overseas students." Rizwan glanced at Rita, scepticism clear in his eyes. Poonam read their expressions.

"That's what she said. She's not the first foreign student there. We know some other women from South Asia who had jobs there."

"Do they have to pay fees?" Rita asked. "Foreign students don't get grants."

"I don't know about that."

"What else can you tell us about her?" Rita said. "Did she have a bank account? A National Insurance number?"

"We were going to apply for an NI number on her behalf. Her employer would need that before she took the job."

"She didn't have a phone," Rita said. "She didn't have an NI number or a bank account. Yet she was an overseas student here." She stared at Poonam, aware the woman was getting more uncomfortable. "Did that not strike you as odd? Do all the South Asian women at the college have a similar background?"

"No," Poonam said quickly. "And that's why Anika stuck in my mind. Most of our clients are British Asians, actually. Some get married and come here. Others are divorcing from abusive partners and don't know their rights. But Anika wasn't like that. She was fresh from India."

Rita focused on Poonam. "What else? You remember Anika for more than her unusual situation, don't you?"

The woman swallowed, and her eyes opened wider. She took out a tissue from her pocket and wiped her mouth.

"She... she seemed in a rush, always. Almost looking over her shoulder. I caught her looking out the glass front of the office, and a couple of times, she lowered her head, like she was trying to hide."

"Did you see who she was trying to hide from?"

Poonam shrugged. "I don't know. When I looked, I just saw the ordinary pedestrians on the road."

"So she was scared?" Rizwan asked. Poonam flicked her eyes at him and nodded.

"When did you last see her?"

"A week ago. I looked in my diary. It was the second of October at two thirty p.m."

There was a knock on the door, and a man poked his head in. His head was mostly bald, with white hair at the back and sides of his pink scalp. He had a kind face, with warm grey eyes.

"Not interrupting anything, am I?" he asked, smiling. Then he came inside and shut the door. He was of medium height, shorter than Rita's five feet nine. He was dressed in a grey vest that looked like a cross between hippie chic and ethnic Indian, and blue jeans. He wore leather sandals on his feet, the kind Rita saw her dad wear when he came to stay with her.

"I'm Paul Manning," he said. "I run the centre here." His face was worn with sun spots, reflecting a life outdoors or in the tropics. His blue eyes were kind, and they crinkled at the corners. "Poonam told me you were coming."

CHAPTER 10

Rita nodded at Paul, a little surprised that a man was in charge of the centre. Paul sat down on a chair near the door.

"I helped set up Roshni as a charity after I came back to England," he explained. "My wife is Indian, and we met while I was backpacking in India many years ago. I was a young man then."

Paul smiled, then glanced at Poonam. "But it's the ladies who run the show. I just stay in the background and sort out stuff with North Yorkshire Council, who provide our funding."

"I see," Rita said. "Roshni has branches, right? I checked your website. You also have offices in Leeds and Bradford."

Poonam said, "And we're opening another one in Hull."

"That's right," Paul said. "We started in Bradford, actually. It sort of grew from there. My wife was the main instigator. When she was busy with our children, I became the chief organiser." He smiled again, warm and genuine. Rita felt at ease in his company. She wasn't getting the same vibes from him as she got from Poonam. Paul seemed more relaxed.

"Have you heard of the woman we're asking about?"

Paul's jaw relaxed, and his eyes lost some of their sparkle. "Yes, Poonam told me. I didn't meet her myself. Are you sure it's her…?" His words trailed off.

Rita nodded. "From the description match, it certainly seems like her. Do you have CCTV here?"

"Yes, in the front office, but not in the rooms. We should be able to get you footage of the woman. What was her name again?" Paul looked at Poonam, who told him Anika's name.

Paul shook his head, a veil obscuring his previous warmth. "It's so sad. We work to help these women, and when something like this happens, we feel we've failed them."

"It wasn't your fault," Rita said. "If we could have that CCTV footage, that would be very useful."

"Of course," Paul said. "We're at your disposal, really. Some of our clients often file PCNs for domestic abuse. We've visited the police station with them, haven't we?" Paul glanced at Poonam, who nodded.

"But nothing like this has ever happened," Paul said. He glanced at Rita. "How did this woman die?"

"That's what we're investigating right now," Rita said.

"Where was she found?"

Rita knew word would spread soon if it hadn't already. Pedestrians and onlookers had noted the crime scene, some before the white forensic tent was erected. She had seen a couple of onlookers take photos. The crime scene was probably on social media already.

"She was found on South Beach."

A soft gasp escaped from Poonam, and Paul closed his eyes, his forehead creasing. "That's terrible. I know the beaches aren't great places late at night, but this is a different level, isn't it?"

Rita was well aware of the drug dealing that had been reported on the beaches at night.

"Yes, I know. That's why we need your help. Hopefully, we can get some answers soon."

"Of course. I'll speak to our security man now and get the CCTV footage for you. Is it okay if he downloads the files onto a removable disk?" He held up two fingers to indicate a small USB drive.

"That would be great, thank you."

"I'll get it now. If there's anything else you need, please don't hesitate to ask." Paul rose and left the room.

After the door shut, Rita looked back at Poonam. "You thought Anika was in trouble, didn't you?"

Poonam looked down at the table, seeming undecided.

"I didn't know what to think, to be honest. We get a lot of vulnerable women coming here—domestic violence victims, single mothers who can't make ends meet. Many don't speak English well, and they don't want their families to know they're here. I don't know if she was one of those."

"And her story about coming from India on her own—was that just something she made up?"

"I don't know." Poonam looked a little helpless. "Sorry."

Rita didn't think Poonam was hiding anything. The woman was open, maintaining eye contact, showing her true emotions.

"And you've not met any women like her recently?" Rita repeated. "This is important, Poonam. Please think carefully."

Poonam lowered her head, thinking. "No. Can't say I have, to be honest."

Rita asked, "Do you have Anika's registration form? That should have her address, even if she didn't have a phone."

Poonam pulled the keyboard towards her and clicked a few times. She scrolled through the computer screen, and then a printer whirred to life under the desk. She handed Rizwan two sheets of paper. The form contained Anika's name, date of birth, and address, but not much else. Rizwan pointed at the photo box in the top right corner of the form. It was empty.

"She didn't have a photo? Like a passport photo?"

Poonam shook her head. "She must have had a passport—otherwise, how did she get into the country? But she said she left it at home."

"How many times did she visit here?"

"Twice, I think. I saw her both times. I checked the register after I spoke to you. She didn't come when I wasn't here—I work four days a week."

"Can you ask the other ladies if they saw her at any point? Maybe out in town or somewhere?"

"Yes, I already have. They haven't. But they'll help spread the word in the community. Someone might have seen her."

Rizwan asked, "When Anika came here, was she alone?"

"Yes." Poonam looked at him and blinked twice. "But like I said, she was always in a rush, and I got the impression she was worried or scared about something."

"Maybe about being here and asking for help?" Rizwan suggested. "I know she was looking for a job, but you help women who are in legal trouble as well, don't you?"

"Yes, we do. We also deal with solicitors' costs, legal aid applications, accommodation—everything, really."

"Maybe job hunting wasn't the only reason Anika came here," Rizwan said. "But I guess we'll never know."

There was a knock on the door, and Paul returned with the USB drive. He handed it to Rita, who accepted it with thanks.

"Would you like to check it now?" Paul asked, looking a touch anxious. "We can always give you more if you need it."

Poonam inserted the drive into the desktop, and they crowded around her chair to look at the screen. Paul stood opposite, watching.

Rita saw a colour screen divided into four sections. Two showed the front and back entrances, while the other two split the view of the front office into left and right. The timestamp read 2:30 pm, 2nd October.

A young woman entered the office. She hesitated for a moment, clutching the strap of her handbag. A receptionist got up, and the young woman approached her. When she turned, Rita asked Poonam to zoom in on her face.

They now had a clear view of the woman's face. Rita could see the elephant pendant necklace on her V-neck and, in another frame, spotted the bangle on her left wrist.

The face looked very similar to the victim's. She wore white trainers, dark brown jeans, and a green jacket.

"That's her," Rizwan said softly. "Anika Joshi."

CHAPTER 11

Grey clouds had scudded across the sky suddenly as Rita and Rizwan emerged from the Roshni office. The wind was fresh, blowing in from over the sea. The tang of brine hung in the air, along with the smell of impending rain. They got into the car, and Rizwan drove to the address on Anika's form.

It was in the southeast part of town, an area called Barrowcliff. They drove down a gridlock of streets with terraced houses packed together like sardines in a tin. Several houses had downstairs windows boarded up, and graffiti adorned the side wall of a corner house. An abandoned mattress lay on the pavement, and the rusting hulk of a car stood on bricks, its tyres stolen for some extra cash.

Children were playing hopscotch on the street, and Rizwan stopped the car to let them move to the pavement. A boy of no more than nine or ten pointed an imaginary gun at them and took shots. Then he sprinted away, joining his friends at football. Rizwan pulled the car over.

"Kids playing, guv, and it's not far. Couple of minutes' walk from here to the end of the road. Shall we walk?"

Rita agreed. Rizwan locked the car, and they bent their heads against the rain and walked as fast as they could. It was a drizzle, whispering against the decaying bricks of the forlorn houses. Rita had seen places like this in

London and, when she was younger, in Scarborough. For a while, Clara and she had lived in a tiny terraced house like this, maintained by the council. She hadn't been to this neighbourhood before, but the signs of poverty were everywhere. Scarborough had never been an affluent town, but Rita felt things had got worse in the last two decades.

Number 34 was near the end of the terrace, where, after a road intersection, the houses began again, stretching to the railway bridge in the distance. Rizwan stopped in front of the door and craned his neck up. The curtains were drawn, and the windows were shut. Patches of damp spread under the windowsills. Plaster had crumbled from the walls, exposing bricks where green plants had sprouted.

Rizwan knocked on the door, but there was no answer. He went on to use his fist to hammer on it, but the result was the same. Rita looked around. To her left, a net curtain twitched in the front window, then a shadow passed across it. She looked opposite, where the curtains were drawn, but the houses were in better shape and looked inhabited.

"What do you want to do, guv?" Rizwan asked. He pushed on the door, which was locked. "I could kick it down."

As this was the last known address of a murder victim, they didn't need a search warrant. Rita thought the door looked flimsy, and a couple of good kicks from Rizwan's heavy boot would make short work of the lock. But that could come later.

"Let's see if there's an alley around the back."

They took a left at the end of the block and walked past a similar row of houses until they came to an alley. It was wide enough for two cars to pass each other. They walked up until Rizwan thought they were at the back gates of number 34. Rita could now hear voices by the fence next door, and she saw smoke curling up. Not far away, a few kids were cycling and kicking a football against a makeshift goalpost.

The back fence door was flimsy, but it was still locked. Rizwan gave it a good shove, and the bolt ripped off the fence post. The garden was overgrown with waist-high weeds. The path leading to the back door was covered in moss. The building looked even shabbier from behind. The roof was still intact, and the back windows were open.

"I don't think anyone lives here," Rizwan murmured as they approached the back door. It was locked. Rita was slightly taller than Riz, and she stood on tiptoes to look in through the kitchen window. It was small, thin and rectangular. The kitchen counters, hob, and sink seemed to be in good order. She noted the light in the microwave and the clean appearance of the white fridge. She took out her extendable baton and flicked it to its full height.

"Open it," she told Rizwan, indicating the back door. Rizwan leaned against it with his shoulder and gave it a few shoves. Then he tried harder. But, like many back doors, it was sturdy.

"Wait," Rita said. Rizwan moved to one side, and she tried the door handle. It wasn't a Yale or Chubb lock, which meant it wasn't a five-lever mortice lock. They were impossible to open without the right key. This was a simple latch-key lock. Rita released a hairpin and knelt by the door.

"Have you got a card?" she asked Riz. "If you slide it through the crack of the door jamb and jiggle the latch, I'll try to snap it through the keyhole."

She inserted her hairpin into the keyhole and fiddled with it, searching for the latch. Rizwan knew what to do. He applied pressure on the latch through the door frame, using his card. Rita angled the hairpin up and down until she heard a tiny snap. She missed it the first time but went back and held the hairpin up. Rizwan slid the card down, and the latch clicked back. Rita pushed the door open.

"Who needs burglars when you have cops?" Rizwan smiled.

The kitchen, as Rita had seen, was relatively well preserved. There was a plate in the sink and some cutlery. The dishwasher had some plates. While Rita checked the kitchen, Rizwan crept inside the house, his baton in hand. Rita took some cutlery in a specimen bag. The fridge had a carton of milk still in date and a half loaf of bread. The cupboards were mostly bare, save for a jar of oats and some quick soup cartons.

Rita checked under the sink for any hiding places but found none. Rizwan called her, and she went to the living room, across the short corridor. A putrid smell of damp and decay hung in the air—the odour of a place with a leaky roof, rising damp, and windows that never opened.

The living room had a black leather sofa with some holes in it, sagging to the left. There was a TV in one corner, opposite the sofa. The shelves were bare, as were the walls.

Rizwan had switched a light on. He pulled the curtains apart. Watery sunlight poured into the room through the net curtains. The carpet was brown and threadbare, the floorboards creaking noisily as they walked around. Rizwan had his gloves on and pulled out a pizza box from under the sofa. It had a couple of crusts in it. He touched one.

"Hard and ice cold. Been here a while."

"So has the air," Rita wrinkled her nose. "Open the window, will you?"

She left the room and tried the front door. It was locked, and no key was visible. There was no telephone here, just an empty socket. Rita looked up the stairs, at the darkness on the landing.

"I'm going upstairs," she called to Rizwan. The steps groaned under her weight. Wallpaper peeled from the walls. The smell of damp and stale air was stronger here. Rita clamped her gloved hand over her face, wishing she had a mask. She paused on the landing. The silence pressed in, broken only by her breathing and Rizwan moving downstairs.

She tiptoed into the first bedroom. The beds looked slept in. When she put a hand on the nearest mattress, it was warm. Someone had been here recently.

Then she looked at the suitcase. Clothes were spilling out: women's underwear, a make-up bag, jeans, cardigans, and two salwar kameez.

Rizwan appeared, a grim look on his face. "A couple more mattresses in the small bedroom. Been used."

Rita stood, a sickness in her heart, mind buzzing. "Let's speak to the neighbours."

CHAPTER 12

Rita went out the front door and knocked on the door to the right. A woman with her hair up in pink curlers, holding an unlit cigarette to her lips, answered. She was dressed in a pink bathrobe that matched her curlers, and red slippers. There was a clamour behind her, and then a little boy appeared, trying to squeeze past her and out through the door. She caught the boy's collar and pulled him back.

"But I want to play," the boy whined.

"Go and play with your sister in the garden," the woman said. "Or I'll cuff you round the ears."

The boy still tried to make for the door, but he saw Rita and stopped. Then he turned around and sped past his mother, back into the house.

The woman lit her cigarette outside the door and blew out a lungful of smoke.

"You a cop?" she asked Rita, her eyes moving up and down Rita's figure.

"Yes," Rita said. "DI Gupta, from the North Yorkshire Police. Did you know the people in number 34?"

The woman stared at Rita, smoking. "Not really. They came and went. No one paid them much attention."

"Who were they? When did they move in?"

The woman shrugged. "I don't know. I saw some women being brought in a car one night, a few weeks ago. They came and went. Never stayed long. Indians, or Pakistanis they were."

Rita took out the e-fit photo of Anika and showed it to the woman. She leaned closer for a look, then frowned.

"Aye. Seen her, I think. She was here recently. Can't remember the last time I saw her, though. A couple of days ago, I reckon."

There was a crashing sound behind her, followed by a wild whoop. She turned and shouted a volley of scolding.

"Look, I've got to go." She put a hand on the door, then her eyes strayed past Rita to the opposite side of the street, where Rizwan was conducting a door-to-door enquiry.

"Eh up. What's happened here, like?"

"We need to speak to the women who lived here," Rita said. "And did you see any men? What about the driver of the car?"

"Aye, there were two blokes, like. One of them drove the car, like you said. Another I saw with that lassie whose photo you just showed me."

"What did they look like?"

"One was Asian. The other was white. The Asian guy I've seen before. Mind you, there's lots of 'em round here."

"Can you describe them? Did they have beards, wear glasses—anything you noticed?"

"The Asian bloke was taller than the white man. He had a light beard, not long. He wore normal clothes, as did the white geezer. The white guy was clean-shaven. I didn't pay much attention, to be honest."

"Thank you, that's very helpful," Rita said and meant it. "What sort of car did they drive?"

"Buggered if I know," the woman said, downturned her lips, and took a deep drag of her cigarette before crushing it against a brick on the wall. She dropped the stub onto the pavement by Rita's feet.

"It was a black car. Not small. Like a four-door saloon. But not one of them big new fancy ones, like a four-door big job."

"Do you mean like an SUV?"

The woman waved a hand in the air. "Yes." Another crash sounded behind her, followed by wailing.

"I've got to go," she said, closing the door.

Rita moved on to the next house, but no one answered. She carried on for the next half an hour. Rizwan joined her.

"Two people opposite saw the women come and go," Rizwan said. "And a tall Asian bloke drove the car."

"That's what I heard as well." Rita crossed the street with Rizwan and knocked on the next house. An old man opened the door slowly. He blinked, then narrowed his eyes.

"You lot the bailiffs?"

"No, sir, we're the police," Rita said. She pointed to number 34, across the street and to their right. "Have you seen anyone who lived in that house?"

"Why? What's goin' on there?"

"We need to speak to the residents urgently. Have you seen them?"

The man stared at Rita for a while. "I've seen one of them, like. A woman. She was at the pub with a bloke."

"Can you describe them?"

"The woman was short. Indian, I think. Or Pakistani. She had long hair. Pretty lass. The bloke was older, in his fifties. Seen him before in the pub. Name's Martin. Lives around the corner. Seen him in the betting shop as well."

Rizwan was scribbling in his notebook. Rita asked, "Do you know Martin's last name?"

"No, just seen him around. This was last week. Friday night, around 8 p.m. I was there to watch the football."

Rita showed the man Anika's e-fit photo. The man leaned closer, eyebrows lowered.

"Aye, I think that's her."

"Thank you. Can you describe Martin?"

"He's a big chap. Taller than me, and wider. Got tattoos on both arms. I think they were havin' an argument in the pub. He was sayin' something, but the woman wasn't listening. She walked out in the end, and he followed her. I didn't see them after that."

"Which pub was this at?" Rizwan asked.

"The Crown and Sceptre, at the end of Blackshaw Road. Less than ten minutes' walk from here. We call it the Crown. It's my regular."

Rita took the Asian man's description, which matched what the woman with pink curlers had told her. Tall, with a light beard, and no glasses. Jeans and black trainers.

Rita thanked him and returned to the car with Rizwan. "Get the uniforms out here. I want the house set up as a crime scene and a door-to-door on every house in the block."

Rizwan got on the radio while Rita sat in the car, checking the map. She found the pub easily enough. When Rizwan finished speaking to the duty team, they got out of the car. The clouds remained, obscuring the light and threatening, but the rain had relented, thankfully.

As they walked, Rita spoke to Richard, updating him.

"I'm upstairs with Traffic now, checking CCTV for the blue van. It's not been seen as yet. Want me to go to the college? I could speak to the principal, find out more about Anika's student life."

"Yes, please. Have you heard anything else from the uniforms about Anika?"

"The posters are all over town. Nothing from the temples or mosques yet—nothing about seeing Anika, anyway. From the name, she strikes me as Hindu, right?"

"That's correct."

"I'll ask around," Richard said. "Then go to the college. See you back at the nick."

They reached the Crown and Sceptre. Two men stood smoking outside. Both were skinheads, wearing tight leather jackets that looked too small. One sneered as Rita walked past, then spat on the ground and muttered an oath.

"Nice place," Rita said as Rizwan opened the door and stepped inside.

CHAPTER 13

The pub had creaky wooden floors that gave way to a dark paisley carpet, worn out by punters' shoes over the years. A barman was serving a couple of old men, both hands resting on the counter. He looked up as Rita and Rizwan entered. The wary look in his eyes deepened as Rita introduced herself and Rizwan.

"We're looking for a man called Martin. Tall, tattoos on both arms. Drinks here regularly."

"Lots of people drink here," the barman said. "Not sure I know a Martin."

"He was here last Friday. Around 8 p.m."

Rizwan pointed at the cameras. "You've got CCTV, right? Can we check the footage?"

The barman straightened. "I don't know how to use it. Let me ask the landlord."

He went to the rear of the bar and vanished through a door. Rita looked around the pub. It was afternoon, but a handful of people were sipping their pints. They looked at Rita curiously, then averted their eyes.

A short, stocky man came up behind the bar with the barman. "I'm the landlord," the short man said. "What's this about?"

"We need to speak to a man called Martin. He was seen with this woman." Rizwan showed them the e-fit photo. Both men frowned as they examined it.

"Never seen her before," the landlord said. He glanced at the barman, who shrugged.

"Can we see the CCTV?" Rita asked. The landlord scratched the back of his neck, then seemed to make up his mind.

"Alright then, come with me."

"You go with them," Rita said to Rizwan. "I'm going to have a chat with the punters."

Rizwan nodded and left. Rita sat down next to an old man by a window, who was gripping his pint glass with big, gnarly fingers.

"Do you come here often?" Rita asked. The old man looked surprised. He had a peaked farmer's cap. He sat back in his chair and adjusted it.

"It's my local, so yeah. Who are you, like?"

Rita told him, and the man narrowed his eyes. "The police, eh? What's happened then?"

"We're looking for a man called Martin." Rita described him, and the old man frowned, the deep lines on his forehead growing thicker by the second.

"Ey up, I know someone like that. I think so, anyway."

"He also goes to the betting shop in the next block."

The old man's forehead cleared. "Aye, yes, I know 'im." His eyes narrowed again. "What's he done then?"

"He was seen with this woman." Rita put Anika's e-fit photo on the table. The man picked it up gingerly, his thick fingers bent with age.

"Pretty lass. You think Martin's done owt to her?" the old man said in a low voice, then looked away suddenly, as if worried he'd said too much. Rita didn't like that.

"Why would you say that?" she asked. "Has Martin been in trouble before?"

But the old man wouldn't talk anymore. He waved a hand. "Be off with yer. I just want to finish me drink in peace."

Rita tried to speak to him again, but the old man was having none of it. She looked around and saw two skinheads watching her. She went and joined them, much to their surprise. They exchanged a knowing look and shifted in their seats.

"Hi, lads," Rita said. She took out her warrant card and held it under the nose of the man next to her. He was big but young, barely in his twenties. He looked at the card and then shook his head.

Rita told them who she was looking for and then showed them Anika's photo. The skinhead curled his lip upwards.

"Too many of them around here," he said.

"Have you seen her, then? With Martin? Last Friday evening, around 8?"

"Nah. Don't know." He looked at his friend, took his drink, and got up. Rita sighed. The skinheads clearly knew something, but unsurprisingly, they wouldn't share it with her. This wasn't getting her anywhere, and she was growing angry and frustrated. Hunger also gnawed at her stomach; she had skipped lunch.

Rizwan came out into the bar area and headed towards her. He looked excited. "I've seen a tall man, ponytail and white T-shirt, arguing with a woman that matches Anika's description. Got it here." Rizwan patted his coat pocket and took out a flash drive. "The landlord admits to knowing who he is, but he wants it to be kept quiet."

They approached the bar, and Rizwan lifted the counter. They went in. The pub landlord was standing inside, next to the stairs that led up. They followed him to the first floor, where he entered an office. He shut the door behind him and took out a tissue to wipe the beads of sweat from his forehead.

"Look, I don't want any trouble. That man on CCTV is a local gangster. His name's Martin Keane. He drinks here, and he's got mates. You didn't get this from me, do you understand?"

"No problem," Rizwan said. "Where does he live?"

"I don't know. But he's here often, so he can't live that far. If you ask around, you might find out."

"How did you know he was a gangster?"

"I've seen him with the dodgy types. They look up to him. He's like their leader. They don't do any dodgy stuff around here because they know about the CCTV."

"Who might know where to find him?"

The landlord spread his hands. "I don't know. Look, it's time you left. I've told you all I know."

Rita stared back at him. "You know that known criminals frequent your place and you do nothing about it?"

The man gulped, his nostrils flaring, patches of colour appearing on his cheeks.

"All I know is what I hear from people."

Rizwan said, "When we asked you, you said you didn't know anyone called Martin. But the CCTV changed your mind, did it?"

The man was sweating now, and his pot belly heaved as he shifted on his feet. "I don't want any trouble. I tried to help you, and this is what I get for it?"

Rita wondered if the man had come across the police before. "Do you have fights in the pub? Or any other hassle?"

"A couple of times. A group of bikers came in, and they didn't like some of the lads here." He looked around, his bulbous eyelids blinking as if someone was hiding in the office. He dropped his voice.

"The bikers had some beef with Martin. I don't know for sure, but I think they were selling drugs here, and Martin and his lads didn't like that."

"Has Martin been in prison?" Rizwan asked.

The man looked reluctant to speak but then nodded. "That's what I heard. For armed robbery once, and then GBH. He came out last year." His face was red now, and he took out a tissue to wipe his forehead. "That's all I know."

"Those skinheads downstairs," Rita asked. "Would they know where Martin might be? Do they work for him?"

The landlord frowned. "I'm not sure. Not seen Martin speak to them."

Rita studied the man. "What's your name?"

"Paul Jenner."

"Have you had any brushes with the law, Paul?"

The man shook his head vigorously. Rita didn't think he was lying. Easy enough to check if he was.

"You've never seen that girl that Martin was arguing with last Friday? Think carefully."

"I might've. I'm not sure. Indian or Pakistani girl, right? There's a big community of them around here. Some of the Asian men come here, but not the women, really." Concern deepened on his face. "Why?"

"No reason. We need to find her, that's all. If you see an Asian man here—tall, light beard, no glasses—then can you please let us know? And keep your eyes and ears open for Martin and the Asian man we just described."

Paul nodded. Rizwan handed him a card. "Call the number at the bottom. No one will know you're calling, okay?"

Paul let out a shaky breath. "You didn't hear any of this from me. I don't want any trouble."

"If you play by the rules," Rita said, "it'll be fine."

CHAPTER 14

Richard walked up the broad stairs of the Scarborough Further Education and Training College. He had never studied there, but he knew people who had.

Richard had grown up in Scarborough and had attended Cranston College, a sixth-form college just outside the town where he had done his A-levels. The FETC, as it was known, didn't provide academic subjects. It was a training school for those who wanted to go into professions like plumbing, bricklaying, or secretarial work.

Fashion and cosmetics had been added to the mix in recent years, and women who left school at sixteen could enrol at the FETC to learn those skills. Like Anika Joshi had, Richard thought, as he walked into the wide atrium.

He couldn't imagine why Anika would travel all the way from Mumbai, India, to study at the FETC of all places. Well, he was about to find out.

Students milled about, and no one paid him any attention. There was no reception as such. He had to stop and ask someone for the administration office, and he was directed to a glass counter halfway down a corridor. A middle-aged woman with pink hair was staring at a screen and didn't look up as Richard stood there. She blew a bubble with her gum and then popped it. Behind her, two women spoke on the phone in a small office. Richard knocked on the glass, and the woman startled. She swivelled her eyes at him, her green irises as wide as a deer caught in headlights. Richard indicated the glass, and she punched a black button on the table next to her. A microphone buzzed to life on the wall above the glass.

"May I help you?"

Richard pressed his warrant card against the glass. "Detective Sergeant Richard Staveley of North Yorkshire Police. I need to speak to the Principal or Dean about a student. It's urgent."

The receptionist gaped at the card, then stood rapidly, pushing her chair back. "Just a moment, please."

She spoke to one of the women at the desk, who had ash-coloured hair and wore glasses. The woman glanced at Richard and then picked up the phone. The younger receptionist came back to Richard.

"Please have a seat." She pointed down the corridor. Richard looked at the atrium and the wide set of doors he had just walked through. Wooden benches were arranged in the corners. On one of them, a group of older teenage girls chatted and giggled.

"How long will this take?" Richard asked evenly. "As I said, this is an urgent matter."

"Not long at all. My supervisor is contacting the Principal." The woman glanced behind her. The ash-haired woman was holding the phone, not speaking to anyone. Her foot tapped the floor, and a nail tapped on the desk.

"I'll be waiting," Richard said. He sat down on a bench that gave him a clear view of the glass counter. He took out his phone and checked his texts. Rizwan had been in touch. They were looking for a Martin Keane, a known criminal. He had been caught on CCTV speaking to Anika. Richard couldn't access the police database remotely, but he filed the name in his memory. He pulled up a map and checked the house where Anika had lived. With any luck, the place was now set up as a crime scene, and SOC were on their way.

He saw a door in the reception office open, and the older, ash-haired woman hurried up to him. She was slim, her spine erect, with a pensive look behind her black-rimmed glasses.

"Mr Lindsey will see you now," the woman said. "Please follow me."

Richard walked after her as she went up the broad stairs to the right and to the second floor. She went through a set of double doors and into a corridor where the brown carpet was softer, the wallpaper had a nice pattern, and framed art posters hung between the windows. She knocked on a brown door and then opened it.

The office was large but modestly decorated. Shelves adorned three walls, lined with books. A tall, broad-shouldered man with a lazy left eye stood to his full height. Well over six feet, Richard guessed—way taller than his own five feet seven. The man stepped out from behind his desk and came forward. He thrust a hand out, and Richard shook his warm grip.

"Daniel Lindsey, Principal at the FETC. My staff said you were a detective, is that right?"

"Yes, that's correct."

"Please have a seat. Jenny," Mr Lindsey called out to the woman as she was leaving, "hold all my calls for the next fifteen minutes."

"You have a meeting with the councillors at twenty past," Jenny said. "That's in ten minutes."

Mr Lindsey glanced at his watch. "Make it twelve and tell them I'm held up in a meeting."

Jenny closed the door softly, and Richard waited until he heard the click. Mr Lindsey adjusted the glasses on his nose. His lazy left eye was disconcerting, but the man had an interested yet anxious look on his face. His gaze, in the good right eye, was sharp, and the way he leaned forward, elbows on the desk, suggested he didn't want this to be bad news.

"What's the matter, Detective? Any of our students in trouble?"

"I'd say so." Richard put the e-fit photo of Anika on the desk and slid it across. "This woman was an overseas student at your college. Her name is Anika Joshi. She was found dead at South Beach in the early hours of this morning."

Mr Lindsey gaped at Richard, his mouth slightly open. He looked down at the photo, then cleared his throat and glanced back up at him.

"Are you sure she was a student here?"

"Yes, positive. We found her student visa."

Richard had used the name and DOB that Rizwan had sent him from the offices of the Roshni Community Centre. He had downloaded Anika's passport from the UK Border Force records, showing when she had arrived in the UK.

"She enrolled four weeks ago," Richard said. "That's according to the information we have, but we need confirmation." He was relying on what Rizwan and Rita had learnt from Poonam at the community centre.

Mr Lindsey was looking at Richard as if he was struggling to process what he had just been told. Richard raised an eyebrow.

"Could you please have a look at your records and check?"

Mr Lindsey nodded slowly. He grabbed a wireless mouse and clicked on his laptop screen. After a few seconds, he blinked and nodded once.

"Her name is here." His mobile right eye flicked to Richard, while the left remained on the screen. "Just her details. I don't know anything else about her, you must understand."

"Can I see that, please?"

Richard noted the reluctance with which Mr Lindsey turned the laptop towards him. Anika's profile picture was on the left of the screen, with her details on the right. Richard scrolled down. She had a student ID number and an address, which matched the location Rita and Rizwan had just visited. But no phone number. He took photos, then requested Mr Lindsey forward the information to him. He gave the Principal his email.

"So you never came into contact with Anika?" Richard asked.

"No. According to this," Mr Lindsey indicated the screen, "she was studying cosmetic fashion and design. She's a new overseas student who joined this semester. That's all we know, I'm afraid."

"And why did she join your college? I mean, how did she hear about it?"

Mr Lindsey cleared his throat. "We have affiliations with some Indian institutions, mainly in the building and engineering trades. They want to train people, and we have the courses."

"And such courses are not available in India?"

"They are," Mr Lindsey said patiently. "But we can offer courses from the Federation of Master Builders. That is attractive to foreign countries."

Richard didn't see it that way, but he kept his thoughts to himself. "But Anika wasn't studying building or engineering. How did she hear about the course in fashion?"

"Presumably from one of our partner institutions. They probably asked her to apply, and she did so." He raised both hands. "I don't know."

As if there weren't enough fashion colleges in India, Richard thought in silence. Why would a country of 1.4 billion people send a student to study at the FETC in Scarborough? It was hardly a renowned college for fashion.

"Overseas students pay fees, don't they? I looked at your prospectus online. The fees for the fashion course are eight thousand five hundred for the first year and then ten thousand for the second. Is that correct?"

"Yes."

"And had Anika paid for the course?"

Mr Lindsey hesitated, and a guarded look appeared in his eyes. "I need to check with Finance. Do you want me to?"

"Yes, please."

Mr Lindsey breathed in deeply and picked up his phone. His fingers moved on the desk as he spoke to someone, then hung up.

"The finance staff will check and get back to me. It shouldn't take long. Is there anything else I can help you with?"

"Yes. To get a student visa from an overseas country, what is the process?"

Mr Lindsey licked his lower lip once. His attitude now was different from before. Richard sensed a change, and his words were chosen with care.

"Well, the student applies to us. We evaluate the application and make a shortlist. Then we conduct a phone or video interview and make another shortlist. The successful applicant gets the place."

"So, for Anika's course, how many candidates did you have?" Richard didn't bother to hide the scepticism in his voice. If Mr Lindsey sensed it, he kept it to himself.

"I can't recall exactly now. I can let you know if you wish."

"On average, how many overseas students do you have every year?"

Mr Lindsey shifted in his seat and cleared his throat. "Across all our courses, I'd say about ten. Some years fewer, some more."

"And in fashion?"

Mr Lindsey held Richard's gaze, then blinked. "I don't have exact numbers. But maybe one or two? That's a guess, but I can send you exact numbers if you want." He glanced at his watch.

Richard wasn't getting a good vibe from Mr Lindsey. The principal had become stiffer, and Richard didn't like it.

"I can see the college earns a reasonable amount from overseas students," he said. "You must know in advance that they have the ability to pay?"

"Yes, we ask for proof of funds and a deposit before they start the course."

Mr Lindsey's phone rang, and he answered. He spoke briefly, then hung up. "That was the finance department. Yes, she did pay her deposit. That's a thousand pounds, and we have proof that she paid."

"And who paid, exactly? Anika herself or her family?"

Mr Lindsey shrugged. "Again, I need to refer to Finance for that. It's not something that I deal with personally."

"I need to see the bank account that the payment came from."

Mr Lindsey hesitated again, and Richard didn't like it. Then the man exhaled, but a new tautness remained in the lines of his jaw.

"Yes, I can ask Finance to forward those details to you. Now, if you'll excuse me—"

"How many days of college did Anika attend?" Richard interrupted.

Mr Lindsey was about to stand up, but he sat down again. Impatience was clear now in his face, and his lips thinned before he spoke.

"Term started on the twentieth of September. Today is the ninth of October. I assume she was attending college, but again, we have to check with her department."

"If you tell me where I can find that, I will make my own enquiries," Richard said, standing up.

As he was leaving, Mr Lindsey cleared his throat. He was standing. "Mr Staveley. How did Anika die? I mean, what happened to her?"

The news would be out soon, Richard knew. And he thought Mr Lindsey had a vested interest in keeping it to himself.

"She was found on the beach. Strangled to death."

He watched as Mr Lindsey paled, his chest seeming to contract. He breathed faster, then his eyes flickered down to the table.

"My God," he whispered.

"You don't know anyone who might want to do this to Anika?"

Mr Lindsey blinked, then his eyebrows met in the middle of his forehead. "No, of course I don't. I didn't know her, did I? I only met her once, at the video interview."

"When was that?"

Mr Lindsey was sweating. He plucked a tissue from the box on his desk and wiped his forehead. His previous suave demeanour had melted like ice cream in the sun.

"Sometime in June this year. That's when we make our final offers. She was in Panjim, Goa, in South India, at her home. Melanie, the fashion teacher, and I conducted the interview. I didn't see her after that."

"But she attended classes here from September?"

"That is correct."

Richard stared at Mr Lindsey, and the principal held his gaze. Then Richard nodded. "If you remember anything, please call me on that number." He indicated the card he had left on the desk, which Mr Lindsey hadn't touched.

Richard went downstairs to reception, where the pink-haired woman at the counter showed him the way. The Fashion and Cosmetics Department, as the name above the double doors proclaimed, was down a corridor on the left, at the end of the ground floor.

The receptionist introduced Richard to a woman who was passing by. The woman startled when she heard Richard's job title.

"Detective? About one of our students?"

"Yes," Richard said. "Do you work here?"

"I'm the head of department. My name's Melanie Peabody. Please come to my office."

When they were seated in Melanie's office, Richard explained the situation. Melanie was in her mid-to-late thirties, attractive, with shoulder-length wavy black hair. She wore a pink cardigan with a matching lilac skirt and heels. She frowned as she listened to Anika's story. Richard didn't tell her how or where she had died.

"You did the interview with Anika, is that correct?"

"Back in June, with Daniel, yes. She was a nice girl, I thought. Her English was good, and she seemed confident. She had a good portfolio of work. She did traditional embroidery of blankets, which she showed us—very colourful. And she had designed dresses. All very interesting. I thought we were lucky to have her."

Melanie's face clouded over. "What happened to her?"

"She's dead, unfortunately. She was found on South Beach. Strangled."

Melanie looked like she'd been slapped. She sat back, mouth open, the colour fading from her cheeks.

"Did you see Anika after she started here? She attended classes from September, is that correct?"

Melanie tried to compose herself. She touched her forehead, looking flustered. "Sorry, this is just so unexpected. Poor girl. Yes, I did see her."

She frowned then, as if something had just occurred to her, but she stared at the floor.

"What did she seem like to you?" Richard leaned forward, aware of the moment.

Melanie raised her head, her eyes troubled. "Anika didn't seem like the woman I interviewed in June. She seemed withdrawn and quiet. She didn't speak much."

"And what was she like in June?"

"Very different. A confident, well-spoken girl, like I said. She was keen on getting a qualification... To be honest, I thought she was too ambitious for us. But—"

"You wanted her as a student."

Melanie nodded. "Yes. But I didn't understand what happened after she got here...She barely spoke to me. She attended the classes, and sat at the rear, looking miserable. I know England can be a shock in October, after the sun in India. But it was more than that. I spoke to her a few times. She was living in the east of town, with a couple of fellow students, she said."

"Did you know these students?"
"No."
"Do you arrange accommodation for overseas students?"
"Yes, we do, but Anika had declined that offer. She had friends here who could arrange accommodation for her."
Interesting, Richard thought. "Did you know who these friends were?"
Melanie shook her head slowly. "Sorry. I now wish I had."
"How did Anika apply? Was she recommended by someone? Friends or family? I'm trying to find out as much about her as I can."
Melanie nodded. "Yes, of course. We get all applications from the central body called UCAS. We just download the applications sent to us. Anika's stood out as she was one of the two overseas students who applied to us. The other lady, May Lee, is from China. I saw her this morning, by the way. She seems to be doing okay."
Richard wrote down May Lee's name and circled it. "What can you tell me about Anika's background?"

"On her application she wrote about growing up in Panjim, which is the capital of Goa. Goa used to be a Portugese state till India liberated the state in 1961. The place has a fascinating history, which Anika evoked in her application. She lived with her family." Melanie stopped and frowned. "I'm sure I have her next of kin's contact details from the application. I can forward that to you."

"Yes please, that would be very useful." Richard gave Melanie his email address and phone number.

He said, "I;m assuming Anika's family came up with the cash for her to attend college here."

"That's what she said, yes. Family savings."

"Can you think of anyone who knew Anika? Anyone who came to see her at the college? Or anyone she spoke of?"

Melanie pressed her lips together as she thought. Slowly, she shook her head. "No, sorry. She kept to herself. Like I said, a total change from the person I met on the video link at interview. She was silent and withdrawn from the first day she attended here. I asked obviously, what the matter was. I thought she was homesick, and God knows Scarborough can be a lonely place for anyone, especially someone moving country."

She lifted the tips of her shoulders, sorrow etched in the corners of her eyes. "But she always told me she was fine. I knew she wasn't, but what could I do? I feel bad now. I should've looked after her better."

Yes, maybe, Richard thought to himself in silence. Questions whirled in his mind. "Is there anything else you can tell me about Anika?"

"I can ask the students in her course if they had any interactions with her. I'm not sure that she did, to be honest. She found it hard to integrate, I guess. But she certainly didn't seem like that when I interviewed her."

"Please speak to the students and let know if you find anything. I'll be in touch."

CHAPTER 15

Rita and Rizwan went for a walk around the neighbourhood after they emerged from the pub. The grey terraced houses, grey pavements, and red-brick tenements reminded Rita of the Scarborough she had grown up in—numerous families stacked in tiny abodes like sardines in a can. A couple of women stood outside their front doors, chatting, and turned to look as they walked past. Rita ignored the looks she got. In these streets, everyone knew one another. She and Rizwan were strangers, and that too in suits. People here knew what the cops looked like. Tongues would start wagging. Curtains twitched in windows as they walked down the street.

"Where are we going, guv?" Rizwan asked.

Rita stopped and rocked on her heels. "Nowhere in particular. Just wanted to get a feel for the place."

The pub was now hidden from view, a block away, around the corner. "We won't find much by asking around here," Rita said. "If Martin is a local gangster, word has already spread that the Old Bill's in town."

"Old Bill," Rizwan grinned. "How very Cockney of you. All those years down south made you a softie, if you don't mind me saying. We call them—I mean us—Feds these days."

"Aye," Rita nodded, a half-smile on her lips. "Feds is also street slang for cops in London. Old Bill is old school now, I suppose. A bit like me."

"You ain't old, guv," Rizwan protested as they walked back. Rita didn't answer; she didn't want to invite a debate on her age. No children or partner, and barely a family. A father, hundreds of miles away. Not bad for her early forties.

They turned right and did a loop around the pub before heading back to their car. The rain started up again as they drove back to the station. Rita picked up coffee and biscuits for the lads and a salad for herself. She helped Rizwan carry the tray back to the office, holding the door open for him.

Richard accepted the coffee with a hearty thanks. "Just what I needed, guv, thanks."

Rita had already spoken to Richard while driving back. "Did you get Anika's application through?"

"Yes, and the finance details. I've got the bank account number that paid a thousand pounds into the college funds. It's an Indian bank, and the name on the account is Mr Sachin Joshi. I'm assuming that's her dad or a male family member. I haven't contacted the family yet."

"Yes," Rita said, taking a mouthful of the chicken Caesar salad. God, she was famished. "Let's hold back on that for now. The family will have questions, and I want to be better prepared. Did her student application have a photo that matches the passport? Well done for getting hold of that, by the way."

"I had to chat up a woman at the Home Office," Richard grinned. "Been a while since I did that."

Rizwan said, "And that too for a passport, eh? Bet you offered to buy her a drink."

"Well, she just heard my deep masculine voice and agreed to my request. When was the last time you did that, son?"

Rita said, "Did you speak to any of Anika's friends or fellow students?"

"They were in lessons, but I did manage to corner a couple in the corridor. They didn't know her. One of them vaguely recalled seeing her in class. That does tally with what Melanie, the head of department, told me. Anika was a changed woman from what she was back home."

"Scared and silent," Rita mused. She put her fork down and drank from the plastic carton of water on her desk. "You said Melanie thought it was a big change."

"Yes. And Anika wouldn't tell Melanie if anything was wrong. 'Scared' is the right word."

"And we know how she lived," Rizwan chimed in. "That house has seen better days. How many of them slept in that bedroom upstairs? At least four mattresses on the floor."

"Five," Rita corrected. "And one was warm. The suitcase had some clothes. Some might belong to Anika."

Rizwan picked up his phone and spoke to Traffic, alerting them to check CCTV with the descriptions of the bearded man and Martin Keane.

"Uniforms have started the door-to-door in Anika's neighbourhood," Rizwan said after he put the phone down. "Not sure if Shola's had the chance to go around yet."

"She might still be busy with the beach crime scene," Rita said. Scarborough was a small department, and Shola had two helpers—Henry and Emily. The beach was a large area to search and take samples from, even with the uniforms helping. "I'll catch up with her soon."

"Passport now on your email, boss," Richard said. "And the student application."

Rita clicked on her keyboard, and the passport came up. For the first time, Rita saw Anika when she had been alive. She had light brown skin, large brown eyes, and long black hair. She was beautiful, with the hint of a smile on her lips. Melanie had been right—Anika's face, even within the constraints of a passport photo, beamed with confidence. This was a bright, happy young woman who had been torn from her family and killed by an evil, cold-hearted bastard. Rage boiled in Rita's veins, and her jaw clenched. She would find who did this to Anika. *That's my promise to you*, she said silently as she stared at Anika's face.

The passport had a one-page student visa clipped to one of the pages, visible on the screen. It was a one-year, multiple-entry UK student visa.

She cleared her throat. "Anika would've applied for this visa from her home in Panjim, Goa. She had the acceptance letter from FETC and sent her letter in. Can we check that application with the British High Commission in Panjim? They should have a copy."

"FETC has sent me the acceptance letter," Richard said. "It's in the attachments I sent you."

Rita had a look at it. The acceptance letter was signed by the principal, Daniel Lindsey.

"What did you think of the principal?" she asked Richard. He leaned back in his chair and rested his hands on his pot belly.

"He's used to being a leader. Good at his job. But as I kept digging into the overseas students, he became more guarded. Almost as if he didn't want to talk much. He hid that, of course, but I didn't get a good vibe."

"What do you mean? He's not telling us something?"

"Yes," Richard said slowly. "I'm not sure what, though. He put me in touch with Finance and Melanie. She was very different. Much warmer, and I thought she had genuine affection for Anika."

Rizwan said, "Something happened between that interview and her arriving here. When she went to Roshni, she didn't even have a phone. No photo ID. And that place where she lived—I mean, what student lives like that?"

"Who owns that house? Have we checked the records?"

"Not yet, guv. I'll do it now," Richard said.

"And the neighbours said Anika and two other women came in a car, driven by two men. And she was seen with that bearded man. We need to get CCTV footage and get that car on ANPR."

"On it, guv," Rizwan said.

"Any sign of the blue van that was seen at the crime scene?" Rita asked.

"Ah yes," Richard said. "It was a rented van from a dealership in Leeds. The driver paid cash, and his name is…" Richard peered at his screen. "Andy Stetson. He's a builder, apparently, and has an address in Leeds. I've not checked it, but I called his mobile. No answer, but I left a message. The van must be off-road. ANPR still hasn't found it."

"Good. Keep looking." Rita checked her phone and saw that Shola had responded to her text from earlier. She pushed her chair back and stood. "I'm going up to see Shola."

CHAPTER 16

Rita went up the stairs to the second floor and rapped on the door marked *Scene of Crime Head Office*. After a few seconds, she heard the click of heels on the floor, and the door was flung open. Shola stepped aside, and Rita entered.

The lab was within the office, with white counters stretching to the windows at the far end. Microscopes, overhead lights, and laptop screens were arranged on the desks. Rita didn't see the lanky figure of Henry or the petite blonde, Emily.

"Have the others gone to the victim's home?" Rita asked.

"Yes. Stretching us thin, aren't you?" Shola raised an immaculate eyebrow on her smooth, shiny forehead.

"Duty calls—what can I say?" Rita spread her hands. "We have a positive ID now, by the way. Her name's Anika Joshi, and she was an overseas student at the FETC."

Rita explained how they had found Anika's name at the Roshni Community Centre and her journey to Anika's home. Shola listened as she led Rita to the desk.

"An overseas student in Scarborough?" Shola looked puzzled. "Leeds or York University, I can understand. But why here?"

"My thoughts exactly. There's something dodgy about it. Richard thinks the Principal's hiding something, and he might be right. Time will tell." She pointed at the evidence bags on the desk. "What have you got for me?"

Shola reached for an evidence bag and held it up. Inside was the gold chain and elephant pendant recovered from the victim's body, along with the gold bangle.

"This is turning out to be more interesting than it looks," Shola began. "At first glance, it's just a simple gold necklace. But when Henry and I cleaned it up, we found this."

With gloved hands, Shola placed the pendant under a microscope. She adjusted the eyepiece so Rita could look.

"See that tiny engraving on the back of the elephant?"

Rita squinted, tilting the eyepiece and adjusting the focus knob, just as Shola had taught her in the past. There, barely visible, were two initials: *A.J.*

"The victim's initials?" Rita guessed.

Shola nodded. "Exactly. It matches her first name."

She continued. "After a bit of digging, we traced the pendant's style. It's a traditional motif—common all over India. I can't be certain without more research, but this piece was almost definitely made in India."

Shola pointed to the gold bangle and stud earrings. "Eighteen-carat gold, so not cheap." She picked up the bangle with a gloved hand, and Rita, also wearing gloves, took it. The gold gleamed under the overhead light. The bangle was a plain circle, but it was crusted with gold ornaments along the top, which ran down the sides. Rita handed it back.

"The problem is, jewellery like this is very common in India," she said. "It's a needle in a haystack. It could have been made here in the UK, but given that Anika had only recently arrived, I doubt it." She puffed out her cheeks. "Still, this is helpful. Any fingerprints?"

"The victim's, and that's it, I'm afraid. No matches with the victim's prints on IDENT-1."

Shola reached for another evidence bag, this one containing a small vial of sand and debris collected from the victim's clothing.

"This," she said, "is where it gets more complicated. We analysed the sand found on the victim. Most of it's typical beach sand—silicon, quartz, and shell fragments—but there's also a mix of industrial particles."

"Industrial particles?" Rita frowned.

"Fine iron ore dust and traces of rust," Shola explained. "Not something you'd expect to find naturally on South Beach. It's more consistent with soil near construction sites or industrial areas."

Rita considered this. "You're saying she had been to an industrial site recently? Otherwise, she'd have washed her hands or cut her nails, and the debris would be gone."

"Yes. But her nails weren't that long. I can't be sure how long these particles had been under them. A couple of weeks? Longer?" Shola shrugged.

Another thought nudged at Rita's mind. Could Anika have been killed somewhere else, like a warehouse, and her body brought to the shore? Or was she killed on South Beach?

Shola had walked ahead to another part of the desk, where a pair of white trainers rested on a tray. They were Anika's. The letters *Paragon* were written in black on the side, though the colour was fading.

"I found the same aluminium and rust particles on the shoes," Shola said.

"Is the iron ore concentration high?" Rita asked.

Shola looked at her closely. "Yes. The rust is minimal. I must say, I've never seen anything like it. What are you thinking?"

"Are there any mines or factories around here that would store iron ore? It's a heavy metal, right?"

Shola folded her arms and crossed her long legs as she leaned against the counter.

"Actually, most of the iron ore we use comes from mines. But it has to be extracted in a chemical plant."

"So it has to be a chemical plant?"

"Or a dolomite mine. Dolomite occurs naturally and contains iron ore, as do several other minerals."

Rita narrowed her eyes. "So if we find a chemical plant that extracts iron ore from other types of soil…"

"You might find where Anika had been recently," Shola finished.

Rita nodded slowly, her mind turning over the possibilities. There was some mining activity in the North Yorkshire Moors—mainly for iron ore, if she remembered correctly. But other metals could be mined there, too. She needed to do some research.

"What about the rest of her clothes?" she asked.

Shola led her to the next counter, where Anika's green coat, blue jeans, and cardigan were laid out. Several areas had been treated with chemical reagents, leaving damp patches.

"Standard cotton and polyester," Shola said. "Fingerprints on them that don't belong to the victim, but no matches on IDENT-1. We're still checking."

"Any sign of a phone?"

Shola sighed. "It's a big beach. Nothing so far. Uniforms have searched the rocks as well. They'll go over it again at first light tomorrow."

It was past 4 pm now, and the light was fading, Rita noted. It was a cloudy day, and the meagre sun was fast being swallowed by the overcast sky.

"The women at the community centre said she didn't have a phone number. I'm not holding out much hope, but you never know. Maybe she had one she didn't disclose."

Shola frowned. "Why would she do that?"

"Not sure. Anika's a strange case. She seemed to have come here of her own accord. She had an interview for the college. But once she arrived, something changed."

"And why here?" Shola gestured around. "For higher education? Surely she should've gone to a well-known university."

"I know," Rita said grimly. "I can't help thinking she was duped into attending the FETC. She might've believed she was going to a very different institution."

Shola opened a folder and slid a close-up photograph of the victim's hands across the desk.

"Dr Das also found blood under her nails—skin cells. It's not hers—her autopsy didn't reveal any injuries consistent with it."

Rita's eyes narrowed. "She fought back."

"That's what we're thinking," Shola said. "The lab's working on a DNA profile now. If we get a match, we'll know who she scratched."

"And even if we don't, we can check it against any suspects we get," Rita added.

Finally, Shola turned to a series of plaster casts lined up on a shelf. "One last thing," she said. "The tyre tracks from the road on the headland above the beach. Bob Chandler, the forensic tyre analyst, sent me these."

Rita examined them. "What do we know?"

"They're from an older van. The tread pattern matches a model that hasn't been manufactured in over a decade."

Rita nodded. "Let's hope we don't find any more victims."

CHAPTER 17

Rizwan was in the office when Rita got back.

"Skipper had to collect his daughter from gymnastics," Rizwan said, referring to Richard. *Skipper* was common slang for sergeant.

He looked up as Rita sat down. "Did Shola have anything interesting?"

"Yes. The victim had iron ore particles under her fingernails. Can we look for iron ore extraction factories nearby? Or anywhere up north, really. Shola seems to think iron ore is mainly extracted from minerals. And there are still some mines in the hills of the Moors, aren't there?"

"Fewer than there used to be," Rizwan said with a frown, "but aye, there are still some. I'll have a look." He shifted some papers on his desk.

"Uniforms got back to us. Door-to-door inquiries have revealed a couple of things. At least three neighbours mentioned men visiting number thirty-four—Anika's house—at night. Random men. The women who lived there were all of South Asian origin. The same brown car that the woman next door told us about was mentioned again by other neighbours. Ditto with the tall, bearded Asian man seen with Anika."

"Did anyone see Anika?"

"Yes. She was seen on the street, and one neighbour also saw her with a man who matches Martin Keane's description. Speaking of whom, I've got his file here. His name search on our database lit up like a Christmas tree."

Rizwan turned his laptop around so Rita could see. The mugshot of a man with a long, hard face and dull grey eyes stared back at her. Not a bad-looking man, but with the rough, grizzled look of an ex-convict—the type Rita knew well. His list of PCNs and convictions was long—armed robbery, drug dealing, grievous bodily harm (GBH), which basically meant he'd beaten someone badly enough to put them in hospital.

"Charming character," Rita said. "How does he make friends with a fashion student?"

"Must be his endless charm and amazing looks," Rizwan said dryly. He pointed at the man's biker jacket. "He looks like a reject from the local Hell's Angels."

"Maybe that's why he fell out with them," Rita said, recalling the pub landlord's story about Martin's fight with the bikers. "Have uniforms found him yet?"

"Nope. He's still in hiding. We've got his address here. He lives six blocks away from the Crown and Sceptre pub—about a ten-to-fifteen-minute walk. He lives alone. No sign of him there."

"If he was the last person to see Anika alive, he's now our prime suspect. Tell uniforms to break in and search. We need to find him. Anything on CCTV?"

"Traffic is about to send me the footage. I'll forward it to you as soon as I get it."

"And the blue van's owner—Andy Stetson?"

"I had a word with West Yorkshire Police in Leeds. They'll send a uniformed team to knock on his door. The DI in Headingley asked us to do it, but I've dealt with him before on a missing person case in Scarborough. He owes me a favour."

"Well done."

Rita looked at her watch. It was dark now and close to 6 p.m.

"Go home. It's been a long day. We have a positive ID, and that's good. Go through the CCTV as soon as you get a chance. We need to find the men involved with Anika—Martin in particular."

Rizwan stretched his arms above his head and yawned. "Alright, guv. What about you?"

Rita sat down heavily in her chair. "I have to write a report for the boss lady. If the CCTV arrives before I leave, I'll take a look. Otherwise, I'm off home too." She shook her weary head and stifled a yawn. "Go on, off you go. I want you here early tomorrow."

Rita walked into the police station's rear car park and waited for her cab. The car park was brightly lit, and a couple of uniformed officers walked past her. She waved at them. Her cab arrived soon after, and she slipped into the back seat, her head resting against the seat, eyes closing as the car drove off.

There was some traffic, but it didn't take her long to reach North Marine Drive, where she lived. Her second-floor flat overlooked Scarborough's South Bay. She had left the curtains open in the living room, and the row of lights glistened like a garland along the promenade. The soft glow shimmered on the sea, and the undulating darkness stretched out into the unknown.

Rita poured herself a glass of white wine from the fridge and sat down in the lounge, putting her feet up. Her thoughts returned to Anika. She had not been alone—Rita was sure of that. The house where she had lived had been used to keep women hostage. Rita suspected they had been forced into sex work. Modern slavery might be at play here. She closed her eyes, the wine slowly unwinding the tension in her head. She needed to find the other women who had lived in that house—before they turned up dead.

She didn't like bringing her work home, but often she couldn't help it. *Obsessive,* someone had called her once. Well, she could only be who she was.

Her phone beeped. It was Jack. She answered.

"I hope you're still not at the nick," Jack's warm voice came down the line.

Rita smiled. The voice hadn't changed in over twenty years, and neither had his unvarying opinion of her. He knew her too well.

"I *do* have a life outside work, you know."

"Does that involve thinking about work at home?"

"Shut up," she laughed despite her tiredness. "Unless you've got anything useful to say."

"I spoke to my friend who runs the chain of restaurants. Samir—his name is—but I call him Sam. He's agreed to speak to you. Says he's got nothing to hide. He might have some information—I don't know."

"Thanks, Jack."

He hesitated. "Are you free tonight?"

"Nope. My social calendar is completely full. You have to ask in advance."

"How about fifteen minutes in advance?"

"Hmm, let me check my very busy diary."

She could *feel* him smiling down the line.

"Can you make some time if I buy you dinner?"

Rita's stomach rumbled at the mention of dinner. Apart from fruit at breakfast and a salad for a late lunch, she'd had nothing to eat all day.

"Perhaps, just this once," Rita said. "Where are we going?"

"Now that would be telling, wouldn't it? I'll be at yours soon."

Rita got up, splashed some water on her face, then redid her minimal makeup. She looked at her hair in the mirror and decided a ponytail would have to do.

Jack knocked on the door. He stood there, looking as handsome as ever in his navy blue suit and dark shirt. She tried to ignore the happy warmth she felt when she saw him—and failed.

"At least you're punctual," she said. "Would you like to come in?"

"Our reservation awaits, DI Gupta. So does your carriage." He indicated his sleek BMW 6, parked opposite her block of flats. "Shall we?"

They drove to Seamer, about ten minutes southwest of Scarborough. Rita knew of it. It was a nice little village with a train station. Posh people lived there—the kind of place her mother and she could never have afforded.

Jack pulled up outside a yellow limestone country pub—a sprawling affair set in landscaped gardens. It looked lovely, well lit in the dark. A black-and-white timber-framed sign hung above the door: *The Blackwell Arms*.

"Been here before?" Jack asked.

"Used to be my local. I know everyone in there—we're thick as thieves." Rita grinned as she and Jack got out of the car.

Inside, a fire blazed in a hearth that took up half the side wall. They were shown to a table in a quiet corner. The place was full, but the lighting was soft and pleasant.

The rest of the evening passed in relaxed conversation. Rita wasn't sure where things stood with Jack. But as they stood at her doorway later, she kissed him lightly on the cheek and gave him a hug.

"Long day tomorrow. Thanks for dinner."

"My pleasure," Jack smiled. "Keep me posted."

She watched as his car disappeared around the corner. Exhaling, she realised she'd been holding her breath. An empty, forlorn sigh shook her from inside, making a question mark in the cold air as it exited her lungs. Then she opened the door and went inside.

CHAPTER 18

Rita didn't sleep well, tossing and turning. Her mother's face appeared in her dreams, as it often did. Clara was shielding someone against the side of a cliff, and Rita was shining a torch on them. Clara's face was twisted with pain, and a howling wind made it impossible to hear what she said.

"Mother!" Rita screamed. "What is it?" She had to get closer, careful not to lose her footing on the rocky cliff. The drop was steep, hundreds of metres down to certain death.

Clara kept moving backwards. Finally, Rita could hear her speak. Clara was shouting, her voice agonised. "They'll take her away. Leave her alone!"

"Who?"

"The girl with me. Don't let them take her away."

"Who? Let me see?"

Suddenly her mother disappeared, and Rita saw Anika sitting on the ground in a white dress. Her head was down, between her knees. Rita called her mother's name, but she couldn't see her anymore. The wind moaned around her, and rain splattered her face. She stepped towards Anika, but the ground began to shake, then cracks appeared. Before Rita could move, the cracks widened, the earth shuddered, and Anika vanished from sight.

"Help me!" someone screamed, their voice trailing into the rain and mist.

Help… Rita woke up, listening to her alarm beep insistently. Her forehead was damp with sweat. She slapped a hand on the alarm and it went silent. It was six a.m. She was glad she had stuck to one glass of wine last night. The dreams got worse when she drank too much.

She always saw her mother's face at night. Sometimes it wasn't even a dream. Clara's memories tormented her—the mother who was her only carer, friend and companion. The only one who loved her, and she was taken from Rita when she was just eleven. The pain never stopped. But at least she had some closure when she came up to Scarborough to open old wounds again, finding her mother's grave.

She got dressed in her jogging clothes, and forced herself to go out. The sun was peeping over the grey and blue sea, and its rays played hide and seek with the cliffs. Rita ran down Marine Drive, heading for the castle and old town. She did a five-mile loop and came back. A quick shower later, she got dressed and left for work.

As she walked to the bus stop, she checked her radio and phone. No messages from work. Her dad had sent a text late last night, and she replied to it. He wanted her to visit him in south Wales for Christmas. It was certainly possible, and it would be nice not to spend yet another Christmas alone.

Rita was in her office by half seven. The others hadn't arrived yet. She sat down to check Anika's social media profile. Anika had several photos on the beach, as one would expect from someone who lived in Goa. She had photos with young people her age, and an older man and woman who looked like her parents. One photo made Rita pause.

Anika was standing next to a man, and her eyes were on him. But the man, standing close to her, was staring straight at the camera. He was older than Anika, but not by much—perhaps a few years. Rita put his age at his mid-twenties. It was his expression that drew her attention. He had a cold, dead look in his eyes, and a light smile that looked more like a snarl.

Rita scrolled through the photos, and saw the man once again. Anika had taken a selfie of the two of them on a park bench. Anika looked her usual, smiling self, but the man's eyes still appeared cold, despite the smile on his lips. It was forced and stretched, not touching his eyes.

The smile of a predator.

Was Rita jumping the gun? Probably. She couldn't find photos of the man elsewhere on Anika's social media. She checked for a tag that might identify him, but frustratingly, he wasn't tagged in either of the two photos.

She took a screenshot of the man and reached for her phone. Shola answered on the third ring.

"Bright and early, Rita? Or is it just my lucky day?"

"As always," Rita said. "Bright and early, I mean. I've got work for you, so I'm not sure about the luck. Can you do a face recognition check for me?"

"And there I was hoping for coffee and cake."

"You don't eat cake. Or biscuits." Shola had an enviable hourglass figure. Rita could only dream of looking like Shola. She knew the woman also had a gym obsession and went practically every day after work.

"I might make an exception for you. Fine, send me the image and I'll see what I can do."

Rita ended the call just as Richard came in. He had bags under his eyes, and he smoothed down his short hair before sitting. He looked tired, and his shirt was creased from yesterday.

"Are you alright?" Rita asked.

"Yes. My youngest didn't have a good night. He's five, and he was sick twice and had a fever. My ex has now taken over his care. I'm a bit worried about him."

"Stay in touch with them, and go when you need to." Rita silenced Richard by raising a hand. "I can always ask one of the uniforms to help. Prioritise your son. Trust me, you'll feel better about it."

"We're already a man—I mean, woman—down with Maggie on leave."

"Doesn't matter." Rita shook her head. "Family comes first." She glanced back at her laptop. "Come and have a look at this chap." She showed Richard the photo of the man with Anika.

"He looks like he's forced to stand next to her," Richard observed. "Weird expression on his face."

"That's what I thought as well. These pictures are in India, by the sea. Must be Goa, or Panjim, the capital, where Anika lived. I'll speak to her family soon, and then I can ask them about this man. I've asked Shola to run a facial recognition scan."

"Great. I'll see if there are any hits on HOLMES or our PCN database." He shrugged. "Long shot, but might be worth it."

The office door opened once again and Rizwan came in, with a steaming cup of coffee. He took off his backpack and sat down.

"Heard back from the CCTV guys, guv. They've got footage ready for us to see. Should be here soon."

"Good. Our priority is to find Martin today. Track his movements on CCTV."

Richard's desktop phone buzzed, and he answered it. After a short conversation, he hung up and walked over to Rita's desk, where she was scanning her emails.

"A witness claims to have seen Anika at an Indian restaurant in town last Friday. She remembers the elephant pendant necklace and gold bangle on Anika, as the witness is a jeweller herself. I just spoke to her."

"What's the restaurant called?"

"The Taj Mahal."

Rita typed in the name, but Rizwan called from his corner.

"I know where that is. It's in town, near the Liquid nightclub. Never been there myself, but I can take you."

Rita checked her watch. It was half eight. "Too early for the place to be open. Do a search and see what you can find out about the Taj Mahal's ownership."

She leaned back in her chair. "If this is true, then why did Anika go to Roshni looking for a job?"

Rizwan looked up. "Maybe she wanted to quit and find another job?"

"Perhaps. But Poonam said she didn't have a job, so I'm wondering if Anika lied about working at the restaurant. That's assuming the witness is correct. I think she is, otherwise she wouldn't remember details like the necklace and bangle."

"She sounded convinced," Richard said. "She didn't speak to Anika, but she's sure about how she looked, especially the jewellery."

"See her for an interview and get a statement," Rita said. "Maybe we can find more witnesses."

Rita pulled out her phone and called Jack's friend Sam, who owned a restaurant. She introduced herself. "DI Gupta speaking. I'm a colleague of Jack Banford. Apologies for the early call. Can you talk now?"

Sam cleared his throat. "Jack mentioned you might call. No problem. What's this about?"

"We're looking into a woman who might have worked in a restaurant called the Taj Mahal, here in town. Have you heard of it?"

"I've heard of it, yes." Sam sounded cautious. "Not great things, I have to say. Their chef used to work in one of my restaurants in York. He wasn't the best, so I let him go. He ended up at the Taj Mahal, or so I heard from one of the managers."

"Does that manager still work there?"

"No, he left. He mentioned they have a high turnover of staff." Sam paused, and Rita sensed he was holding something back.

"What does a high turnover of staff mean? Poor working conditions?"

"I suppose so."

Rita had had enough. "Mr Singh, this is an urgent police matter. If you know anything about that place, please tell me now."

Sam spoke more slowly. "I don't want you to tar all Indian restaurants with the same brush. But some don't pay their staff well. Others don't use fresh ingredients. I don't know much about what goes on inside the Taj Mahal, but I can tell you it caters to the lager louts who stagger out of pubs and nightclubs. My establishments are more upmarket. I'm hoping to open a second restaurant in Scarborough, because frankly, the competition there is poor."

"Do you know the owner?"

"No. Akash, the manager who left, said his name was Yosef Musa. That's all I know."

Rita wrote the name down and circled it. She thanked Sam, ended the call, and told the lads about Yosef.

"I've got his name here," Rizwan said, staring at his screen. "He's the director of a company called Crescent Holdings. Hang on while I check the filings."

Rita let him work, then opened the CCTV footage Traffic had sent over. She called Richard to join her. On Rita's screen, the colour footage was divided into four boxes. The view showed pedestrians on Anika's street in Barrowcliff, where it joined the main road. Rita pressed play, and they watched until Anika appeared, her figure highlighted.

They could only see her face properly when she stopped at the end of the street. Rita switched to another view, and Anika was clearer now. She wore a green jacket and black jeans—the same white trainers she was found in were on her feet. The timestamp read Friday, 4th October.

Rizwan came over. "I can't get Yosef's home address," he said. "But I know where the company office is."

Rita nodded, her attention on the screen. "We found Anika on Monday, 7th October. Is this the latest footage they have of her?"

"Yes, guv," Richard replied. "That's what Traffic sent. They're still checking the rest."

Rita resumed the footage, and they watched as Anika walked to the bus stop and waited. Rita zoomed in, watching her scroll on her phone.

"So she did have a phone," Rita said. "We need to find it—unless the killer took it."

"Uniforms will be searching the beach again today," Rizwan said. "Strange how she told the people at Roshni she didn't have a phone."

Rita shrugged, though a concern was growing in her mind. Anika wanted to stay off-grid. Why?

The bus arrived, and Anika got on. "Number 281," Rizwan noted. "That goes into town."

It was five p.m. Rita guessed Anika was heading to work. The next CCTV footage showed her arriving in the town centre. Again, the camera tracked her in a yellow highlight. She walked down the High Street, then turned down a side street towards a row of shops. On the wall was a white sign with big green letters reading Taj Mahal. Anika went in through a side door and disappeared from view.

Rita clicked on the next file. The timestamp said half past midnight on Saturday, 5th October. Anika emerged again, this time with another person—a woman slightly taller than her, slim build. Rita zoomed in on the woman's face, but the footage was too grainy to make out details, beyond the fact she was probably of South Asian heritage, like Anika. The two walked down the road, then a car swept into view, brake lights glaring.

They stopped, apparently talking to the driver, who remained inside the car. Anika climbed in while the other woman stayed on the pavement. The car sped off, heading out of town.

Richard spoke up. "Traffic says the car's on ANPR. It belongs to a man called Gary Faulks. He's got previous for assault and burglary, and he served six months last year."

"Is it the same car the neighbours saw?" Rita asked. "They mentioned a brown saloon."

"I need to confirm," he said.

Rita nodded, shifting her focus back to the video. The other woman ran into an alley and vanished from view.

"I want to know who that woman is," Rita said. "She might be Anika's friend, and she probably worked at the Taj Mahal."

CHAPTER 19

The beach was cordoned off now, blue-and-white police tape fluttering in the salty breeze. Officers in high-visibility jackets milled about, keeping an eye on passing pedestrians. Yet they remained oblivious to the figure watching them from afar.

Hidden among the dunes, just beyond casual view, the Watcher crouched low, binoculars pressed against his eyes.

There she was. His work. The girl in the sand. *His girl in the sand.* Anika.

Even from here, he could see her motionless form shrouded by a sheet, with a flurry of activity around her. The pathologist stood nearby, his expression grave, gesturing towards her neck. The Watcher wondered if they had found the bruises yet—the delicate impressions of his fingers. They would, of course. That was the entire point.

She had fought him, clawed at his arms, but that had only made the moment sweeter. The desperation in her eyes had given way, at the end, to something else—acceptance. Peace. He liked to imagine she understood, in those final seconds, that he had saved her.

He adjusted his binoculars, his lips curving into a faint smile. Now they were treating her with such care, as though she had meant something in life. She hadn't. None of them did, until he bestowed meaning upon them. He had elevated her. Taken her from the squalor of her existence and preserved her forever in that pristine pose.

And now the police scurried around like ants, trying to work it all out. But they wouldn't.

They never did. He was always one step ahead.

He watched them for a few minutes more. Then he heard voices behind him and froze. He had chosen this spot carefully, out of sight of casual beachgoers. But every so often a randy couple, or a dealer, managed to wander past. He peered over his shoulder but saw no one. The voices receded, and he relaxed, returning his gaze to the beach.

The black-haired Detective Inspector had gone. When she arrived on the scene earlier, his heart had quickened. She was clearly in charge, commanding the others, and even at a distance, he could tell she was the one giving orders. Through the binoculars, he had memorised her features when she turned around. He smiled. This was good. The game had begun.

He lingered a moment longer, then decided it was time to leave. Staying too long was risky. He could always come back after dark. A swift glance assured him no one was approaching; then he got up, slipped on his sunglasses, pulled his hat low, and headed home.

His house was of medium size, unremarkable from the outside, but meticulously tidy within. He prided himself on a pleasant living space. The living room boasted Asian-inspired décor—a mah-jong sofa with round cushions and an ivory coffee table inlaid with small ruby stones that gleamed in the light.

He stepped in and locked the door, then methodically checked the ground-floor doors and windows, as he always did, to ensure there was no sign of a break-in.

He placed his binoculars carefully in their case before going to the bathroom to wash his hands, scrubbing them with near-fanatical thoroughness, as if erasing invisible stains. This ritual was important—like most of his habits—and he worked his fingers methodically beneath the scalding water.

Afterwards, he made himself a cup of tea and settled in the living room. The walls displayed paintings from India, Thailand and Vietnam—places he had visited. Small frames holding original artwork from these countries decorated one side of the room.

His favourite ornaments sat on a shelf near the window: a collection of elephant figurines, some carved from wood, others from stone—some polished and smooth, others rough-hewn. He traced a finger over the largest figure, then replaced it with precise care. Anika's elephant necklace had piqued his interest in these creatures; he had recently learnt that the largest elephant sanctuary was in Sri Lanka. He planned to visit Sri Lanka and India again one day. Perhaps he would find more women like Anika there.

He had no doubt.

Another notable feature of his flat was a corkboard in the corner of the living room. Pinned to it were photographs, newspaper clippings, and hastily scribbled notes, all arranged with meticulous attention to detail, forming a tangled web of faces, dates and locations. Anika's face stood out—the photo one he had taken himself.

"Anika," he murmured softly, brushing his fingers across the picture as though it were a relic. "You were special."

But her role was done now. He had saved her. It was time to find someone else—and he already knew where to start.

CHAPTER 20

Rita ran into Rizwan in the station canteen. He wore a cheeky grin.
"I fancied a slice of cake," he said.

"Enjoy it while you can," Rita replied dryly. "Once you get to my age, a slice of cake becomes a luxury."

"I've got news about the mines in the area," Rizwan said, taking a small bite of his cake. "There's an iron ore extraction site in the North York Moors. It's actually a dolomite mine, but iron ore and tungsten are extracted from the dolomite rock strata."

"Good work, Riz. Where exactly is this mine?"

"In Rosedale—about half an hour's drive from the town centre."

"Send a uniforms unit over to investigate. Let's see if there's any link to Anika or her final movements." She glanced at her watch. It was just after eleven. "Have you heard anything back from the Taj Mahal restaurant or from Yosef Musa?"

"Not yet, guv. But the restaurant or its office should be open by now."

"I want to speak to them soon. But first, we need a proper timeline of Anika's last movements: where she was before ending up on the beach, and why. I'm off to Traffic to speak to the duty sergeant. Get the uniforms out to the mine and keep me posted."

Rita grabbed a coffee and headed upstairs, where she found Shelly, one of the Traffic sergeants, at her desk. Rita had got to know Shelly over the past few months. Shelly had a teenage son with ADHD and had had to withdraw him from mainstream schooling due to behavioural issues. Shelly had confided in Rita during a case, and they had grown close since then.

"Let me run that again," Shelly said, tapping her keyboard. "I know we checked the beach and the restaurant area before, but it can't hurt to have another look. Which restaurant was it?"

"The Taj Mahal," Rita reminded her.

Shelly ran Anika's image through facial recognition, checking footage around the Taj Mahal and along the seafront. They found Anika at the restaurant's door on Saturday, 5th October, but not on Sunday or Monday. The beach cameras drew a blank.

"Part of the trouble is these blind spots," Shelly explained. "You saw that blue van only because there's a camera aimed at the road, not the beach itself."

Rita frowned at the feed. It emphasised yet again that the killer had chosen his dump site carefully—between CCTV coverage zones. Thorough planning to avoid detection.

If he was that careful, would he really risk being spotted in a blue van?

Shelly kept scrolling. Eventually, she stopped. "Here you go: Monday, 7th October, in the morning." She pointed at the screen.

They watched footage of Anika leaving her house and walking along the main road. Cars sped past, and Anika glanced nervously behind her more than once. Then she crossed the road and re-entered the Barrowcliff estate.

Another camera angle showed her pausing at a house and knocking on the door. It opened, and she stepped inside. The footage was grainy, but Rita recognised the street as the one where Martin Keane lived. That meant Anika had gone to see him on the morning of her death. She must have been close to him.

"That's a big help," Rita said, patting Shelly on the shoulder. "Anything else?"

Shelly kept searching with Anika's face and found images of her outside the FETC college two weeks earlier, and on several dates in September—the period when she first enrolled, Rita presumed. Anika appeared alone in all of them.

Rita thanked Shelly, who promised to email the footage. Down in CID, she found Richard setting down his phone.

"I've just got through to the Taj Mahal. The manager's there and says he'll speak to us. He doesn't know where the owner is, though."

Rita picked up her warrant card and radio. "Right, let's get over there." Then she pointed to Rizwan. "Head to Barrowcliff and back up the uniforms looking for Martin, or anyone else who might be involved."

Rizwan nodded. "I've told the team to check the Rosedale mine. It's disused and not safe at night, but Inspector Bennett knows the place well. He'll send a patrol to have a look."

"Tell him thanks from me," Rita said.

She and Richard left for the town centre. Within minutes, they arrived at the street running parallel to the High Street. Rita recognised the white sign with bold green lettering announcing *Taj Mahal*. No doubt the manager or owner would be lying if they claimed Anika had never worked there—CCTV evidence was too strong.

Richard knocked on the door. It was locked. The tinted glass prevented Rita seeing inside, so she cupped her hands against it. She could make out tables, chairs and white tablecloths. At the back of the restaurant, a small light appeared brighter when a kitchen door opened and a short man emerged.

The front door swung open to reveal the same man: plump and pot-bellied, looking distinctly uneasy. Richard showed his warrant card.

"DS Staveley. We spoke on the phone. Are you Sachin Agarwal?"

"Yes, I'm the manager here," the man replied. "Come in."

They stepped inside, and Sachin shut the door. Leading them to a table near the bar, he gestured for them to sit. Richard produced a passport photo of Anika and slid it across.

"Do you recognise this woman?"

Sachin studied the photo; Rita watched his reaction. He looked up, blinking. His balding scalp glistened slightly in the dim light.
"What about her?" he asked. His English was accented, his pace deliberate.

"Have you seen her here?" Richard pressed.

Sachin's gaze flicked warily between them. Eventually, he inclined his head. "Yes. She worked here. Her name's Anika."

"When did you last see her?"

"Saturday night. She worked her shift and then went home. She wasn't scheduled Sunday, and we close on Mondays and Tuesdays."

"How long had she been working here?" Richard asked.

"Just a few weeks—late September, I think. She only did two days a week: Friday and Saturday, sometimes Sunday if we were busy. Evening shifts."

Rita noticed Sachin's foot tapping on the carpet as he spoke. The moment his eyes flicked to her, the tapping stopped. She intervened. "Did she have a contract?"

Sachin swallowed, his Adam's apple bobbing. He hesitated. "She was self-employed. So no formal contract."

"And how did you pay her?"

Another pause. Rita could see he didn't want to incriminate himself. Richard stepped in smoothly. "We're not interested in any unpaid taxes right now. This is a serious police inquiry. You can help us, or we can arrest you for obstructing an investigation. Your choice."

Sachin's features remained tense. It took him a moment, but he gave a curt nod. "We paid her in cash."

Richard noted that down. "How exactly did she get the job?"

"We advertise in local papers," Sachin said, his gaze drifting around. "She replied to one of our ads."

His evasive manner told Rita there was more to it. She let the silence hang, forcing him to fill it. After a few taut seconds, he caved.

"We do advertise in the papers," he repeated. "But sometimes our… business associates supply staff as well."

"What associates?" Rita demanded. "Names. Descriptions."

Sachin opened and closed his mouth. He dabbed sweat from his forehead with a tissue. "My boss would know. I don't—"

Rita cut him off sharply. "We need a name, Sachin. *Now.*"

He sighed, defeated. "There's a man called Rafik. He brought Anika. Rafik knows my boss, Mr Musa."

"Yosef Musa?" Rita asked.

Sachin flinched as though the name itself scared him. "Yes. But I don't want trouble. I'm just a manager—"

"You'll get into far more trouble if you lie," Rita said. "Describe Rafik. Age, height, clothing—anything."

"He's tall, has a light beard with a scar under it on the left side of his face. Sometimes wears a black baseball cap."

Rita glanced at Richard, who nodded. That fit the description of the man seen in the street near Anika's house. "What's Rafik's surname?"

"No idea," Sachin said.

"How often does he come in?"

"Whenever he likes. He brings waiters, kitchen staff… I don't ask questions."

Rita's gaze bored into him. "But you have a good idea what goes on?"

Sachin's breath quickened. "I really don't," he insisted. "Please, can we stop this now?"

Movement caught Rita's eye. Behind the bar, a slight, frail woman had just darted through, collecting something before hurrying off to the kitchen again. She reappeared with a tray of glasses, stealing a glance at Rita. Their eyes briefly locked, and the woman immediately looked away, speeding back to the kitchen.

Rita turned to Sachin. "Who was that?"

He looked over his shoulder at the closing door. "One of the staff. I didn't see who."

But there was something about her that made Rita's heart jolt—a familiarity in her posture or expression. She suddenly realised it was the same woman caught on CCTV with Anika, just before Anika got into Gary Faulks's car.

"I want to speak to her," Rita said firmly. "Fetch her."

Sachin paused, as though judging whether he could refuse. Fear got the better of him, and he stood with a nod, disappearing into the kitchen.

A few moments later, the woman emerged, hovering near the kitchen door. She stared at Rita and Richard, not advancing until Rita beckoned her over with a reassuring gesture.

"Come on," Rita said softly. "Don't be afraid."

Slowly, eyes darting warily about the room, the woman approached. She stopped beside the bar, still watching them.

"Have a seat." Rita indicated the chair opposite where Sachin had been sitting. The woman lowered herself, back ramrod-straight, her face taut with apprehension.

CHAPTER 21

"What's your name?" Rita asked gently.

"Priya."

Rita nodded and introduced herself and Richard. Priya's eyes widened, and her jaw clenched.

"What's your full name?"

"Priya Malhotra."

"Thank you. Did you know Anika Joshi, who worked here?"

Priya didn't reply. Instead, she turned her head slightly to the left, her eyes flicking towards the kitchen door. Rita followed her gaze and caught a glimpse of a head ducking out of sight—Sachin, the manager.

Priya looked back at Rita. Her lower lip trembled, and her long eyelashes dipped.

"What happened... where is Anika?"

"When did you last see her?"

"Saturday night. We worked here." Priya hesitated, and Rita could sense her fear.

"Nothing you tell us will go any further," Rita reassured her. "No one will know. What happened after you left this place on Saturday night?"

"We went home." Priya spoke quickly, as though reciting a prepared response. Had Sachin told her what to say? Or was she simply too afraid to speak?

"Think carefully, Priya," Rita said in a low voice. "We can protect you. Tell us what happened that night."

Priya's nostrils flared as she stared back at Rita, her tension evident. Fine lines creased the corners of her eyes and mouth. Her pale brown skin was slowly mottling into a deep crimson.

"Nothing. We went home."

"So, you lived with Anika?"

"Yes."

"In Seaforth Street, in Barrowcliff. Number thirty-four. Is that correct?"

Priya inclined her head without speaking.

"How did you get to the UK?"Priya opened and closed her mouth before answering. "I came to study at Scarborough FETC—Design and Fashion Technology. I'm here on a student visa, but I can also work. No more than twenty hours per week."The words tumbled out, as though she had been holding them back. Rehearsed. Someone had told her what to say if the police came knocking. Rita's hackles rose. She glanced at Richard, who also recognised the pattern. The FETC, the overseas students, and the restaurant—this was no coincidence. Coincidences were as rare as hen's teeth in Rita's line of work.

"Did you come from India with Anika?"

"No. I'm from Mumbai. I met Anika here."

"Where exactly? At the FETC? Or at the house?"

"At the FETC."

"Who arranged your accommodation?"

Priya froze, her eyes widening. She was struggling now. Rita repeated her reassurance.

"We can protect you. Just tell us who put you in that house in Barrowcliff."

Still, she didn't speak.

"Was it Rafik?" Rita asked.

Priya inhaled sharply, fear flickering across her face like ripples in a pond.

"Or was it Yosef Musa?"

Priya shook her head, then lowered it, staring at her hands. When she looked up again, Rita saw pain in her eyes.

"What's happened to Anika? Why are you here?"

Rita and Richard exchanged a glance. Rita gave Richard a brief nod, and he spoke.

"Anika's dead, Priya. We need to find out who did this. You can help us."

The colour drained from Priya's face. She sat motionless, eyes fixed on Richard, lips parted as if she had forgotten to breathe.

"Help us, Priya," Rita urged gently. "In return, we can offer you protection. How can we contact you outside of this place? Do you have a phone number?"

Priya remained silent. But she didn't need to answer—Rita had already spotted the CCTV camera in the top left corner when she walked in. Someone could be watching them right now.

Keeping her hands below the table, Rita discreetly dropped one of her cards onto the floor.

"Don't look now," she said casually. "But I've left a card by my feet. When you clean up later, pick it up. It's got my number. Call me, okay?"

Priya blinked. Rita saw understanding in her eyes.

"How often does Rafik come here?"

"Not sure. Now and then. He doesn't have a routine."

"But when he does, does he bring someone with him?"

Priya hesitated, weighing her response. Something had shifted within her. She trusted Rita more now. But wariness remained in her eyes, mingled with a new emotion—sadness.

"Often, yes. But not always. Sometimes he just meets with the boss—Yosef."

"Is Yosef here now?"

Priya shook her head. "I don't know." Her gaze slid to the left, then back to Rita. "Stairs go upstairs through that door." She scratched her neck and tucked a loose strand of hair behind her ear.

Rita looked behind them. There was a sink, and next to it, a door. Since arriving, she hadn't heard any creaking above. If someone was upstairs, they were staying very quiet.

Richard asked, "How exactly did you get to the UK?"

Priya stared back at him. "I took a flight from Delhi to Manchester. Then the staff brought me here."

"What staff?"

"The people who organised my student visa and helped me travel here."

"And who exactly are they?" Richard left the question hanging.

Priya looked down at the table. Rita knew this was important. Priya shrugged, her eyes still downcast.

"Just some people back home."

"The same people who got Anika here?" Rita asked.

Priya looked up at Rita. In silence, she nodded. Then she stood abruptly. "I have to go now. I've got work to do."

"Wait," Rita said, lowering her voice further. "I know you're scared. But you're going to be okay. Call me tonight, all right?"

Priya nodded, then disappeared into the kitchen.

Rita and Richard stood as Sachin reappeared from the kitchen door.

Rita pointed towards the ceiling. "Where's the staircase?"

Sachin blinked as though she had spoken in a foreign language.

Rita's tone hardened. "I want to go upstairs. Now."

Sachin gaped. "But there's no one up there. I don't have the keys."

"We can always return with a warrant."

Sachin flustered. "I can show you the stairs, but there's a door upstairs. It's locked. Only Mr Musa has the key."

So that was why there was no sound from upstairs.

"Show me the staircase."

Sachin led them past the sink and through a small landing to a door that opened onto the street. Beyond it, a staircase led to the upper floor. Sachin confirmed that Mr Musa often used this entrance, avoiding the front of the restaurant.

Richard climbed first. At the top, he tested the handle. "Chubb lock, guv. We're not getting through this."

They returned downstairs.

"Is anyone else here?" Rita asked.

"There's a sous-chef, but he hasn't arrived yet. The rest of the staff will be here soon."

"Did you know Anika well?"

Sachin hesitated, then shook his head. "Like I said, she was only here for a short time." His curiosity seemed to get the better of him. "What happened to her?"

Rita met his gaze. "She's dead."

Sachin looked winded, struggling for breath.

Rita stepped closer. "If there's anything else you know about Anika, tell us now. This is a murder investigation. If we find out later you've been withholding information, that won't look good for you."

Sachin trembled. "I swear, I don't know anything more."

Rita let the silence hang before finally turning away. She wasn't convinced. Not yet.

CHAPTER 22

Rizwan was sitting in the unmarked police car opposite the Crown and Sceptre pub when his radio crackled. He answered—it was Rita.

"Receiving, guv. Martin's been spotted in the area by a witness walking her dog. He's not at his house—we've got an undercover unit stationed there. He was seen two streets away from the pub, so we're waiting here. Any updates?"

"Yes. I went to see Shelly at Traffic. Anika saw Martin on Monday, 6th October—the day of her death. He's our prime suspect now."

"Let's see if we can find him, guv. Did you go to the Taj Mahal?"

"Yes." Rita quickly summarised what had happened at the restaurant.

"So this Rafik guy sounds like the bearded man seen with Anika, right?" Rizwan asked.

"Yes. Keep an eye out for him as well."

"Roger that, guv."

Rizwan put the radio down. Sat in the driver's seat was Sergeant Matt Busby, also in plain clothes. A uniformed unit was parked behind the pub in another unmarked car.

A pair of skinheads walked past, both in black leather jackets and combat boots. Rizwan recognised them from before—it was the same pair. They crossed the street, pausing briefly to look around before stepping inside the pub.

From the left corner of his vision, Rizwan saw another man approaching. Medium height, skinny, with a hood pulled low over his face. When he turned to glance across the road, Rizwan noted the dark sunglasses concealing his eyes.

The man's gait was familiar. Rizwan sat up straighter and nudged Busby.

"I think that's him—Martin Keane."

Busby turned the black knob on top of his radio and spoke into it, alerting the other teams.

Rizwan watched closely. Martin was walking casually, not in a hurry, but it was an act. He kept stopping, turning back to check if he was being followed. He hadn't spotted Rizwan and Busby's car.

"He's going inside the pub," Busby said.

"He might not. He knows there's CCTV inside," Rizwan replied.

He was right. Martin walked past the pub, talking on his phone. As he did, one of the skinheads from earlier came outside and hurried over to him. This time, he had taken off his leather jacket.

"Are you sure it's him? Shall we grab him?" Busby asked.

"Wait. Let's see what he does," Rizwan said. He wanted to see who else Martin interacted with and whether he had access to a car.

After a brief exchange, the skinhead turned and went back inside the pub. Martin continued down the road before turning left into a side street.

Rizwan and Busby got out and followed.

Busby spoke into his radio, alerting the other units so they could surround Martin's location.

Rizwan picked up the pace, then broke into a run. He was just in time to see Martin stopping in front of a car, pulling out his keys.

"Stop!" Rizwan shouted.

Martin looked up, still wearing his sunglasses. He hesitated for an instant—then bolted.

Rizwan and Busby set off in pursuit. From the opposite end of the street, two uniformed officers appeared.

Seeing them, Martin changed direction, running into the front garden of a house on his left. He vaulted the low fence but lost his footing, stumbling. He scrambled up and climbed the gate leading to the side entrance. He had just managed to hoist himself over and jump down the other side when Rizwan reached the spot.

Martin sprinted down the side alley and into another garden. Rizwan clambered over the gate after him, the uniformed officers close behind.

In the next garden, a woman stood frozen in front of a shed, a basket of clothes in her hands. Martin was already halfway over the back fence by the time Busby helped Rizwan over.

Rizwan landed hard, hearing the sudden, furious barking of a dog. A German Shepherd shot out of the rear patio door, sprinting towards him.

Rizwan tried to sidestep, but the dog leapt at him, its front paws pushing against his chest as it barked wildly.

"Get him off me!" Rizwan shouted.

The owner appeared, yelling commands, and finally yanked the dog away.

Rizwan took off down the alley, cursing as he saw another locked gate ahead. He climbed it, with the constables following behind.

When he landed on the other side, he saw a uniformed officer wrestling with a struggling figure on the ground.

Martin.

He managed to shake off the officer and got to his feet again, running towards a row of terraced houses.

A group of children were playing hopscotch on the pavement.

"Stop!" Rizwan shouted, not wanting anyone to get hurt.

As Martin ran past, one of the kids—holding a sturdy tree branch—thrust it at his legs.

Martin yelped, lost his balance, and hit the ground hard.

Rizwan was on him in seconds.

Before Martin could move, Rizwan pressed his knee into his back, pinning him to the road. Martin thrashed, snarling and cursing.

The constables arrived, helping Rizwan restrain him. Rizwan forced Martin's hands behind his back and snapped the handcuffs on.

Panting, he wiped sweat from his brow.

"Martin Keane, you're under arrest for the murder of Anika Joshi."

CHAPTER 23

Rita and Richard sat in front of the Principal of the Scarborough FETC, Daniel Lindsey. They had dropped in unannounced, and Richard knew the way to his office. He had knocked on Mr Lindsey's door. The principal was as happy to see him as an antelope welcoming a hungry lion.

"Can we have a word, please?" Richard said. "My boss, DI Rita Gupta, is also here. It's urgent."

Lindsey was half-standing, and he drew himself to his full and imposing height. He was a big man, but his eyes were pensive and anxious. His hands wrung together.

"What's this about? I mean, I have a meeting…"

"This won't take too long."

Richard held the door open for Rita, who walked in and flashed her warrant card in front of Lindsey. The principal peered at it, then at Rita. His cheeks were pale, and behind the glasses, the lazy left eye looked like it was desperately trying to straighten itself—and failing.

"I don't think you made an appointment, Inspector…"

"Gupta, of the Major Crimes Unit, North Yorkshire Police. We're investigating the murder of Anika Joshi, who was a student here."

Rita sat down, and so did Richard. Slowly, Mr Lindsey followed suit. He licked his lips, and his head swivelled in slow motion from Rita to Richard.

"I believe I've told your colleague everything I know. Is there anything else?"

Rita had done some research on the marketing material the FETC was producing in India. It wasn't hard to get hold of online. She pulled out her phone and slid it across the table. Mr Lindsey adjusted his glasses and looked at the screen.

Rita said, "Your online prospectus in India says you have a three-year degree course in Fashion, which clearly, you don't. You have a two-year NVQ, or National Vocational Qualification."

Mr Lindsey looked up, his lazy left eye still stuck somewhere to Rita's left, at Richard.

"This has nothing to do with us, or me personally. This is under the control of our Indian colleagues."

"Who get their marketing material from you. We checked with the university in India you claim as your partner. They were very surprised to learn there are no degree courses at the FETC."

Mr Lindsey spread his hands. "That's their mistake, not mine or ours."

"They get all their information from you, so how could they be operating without any input from you?"

Mr Lindsey shrugged, but with every passing second, his confidence was slipping like a snake moulting its skin.

"But it's not just that," Richard said. "The candidates who are applying think they are going for a degree course. When they apply for their student visa, they need to show a letter of admission to—you guessed it—a degree course. And who signs that letter from the FETC?"

A bead of sweat trickled down Mr Lindsey's sideburn, and he wiped it.

Richard pulled out the folded piece of paper that had been faxed to him that morning from the Home Office. Mr Lindsey looked at it briefly before turning away.

"There's some kind of mistake. I didn't sign that letter."

"Even though it has your signature and comes from this institution?"

"Clearly, someone has forged my signature."

Rita spoke up. "Why? You put your career and reputation on the line for this. Either you did it for money, or they have some other hold on you."

The left eye seemed to twitch, and Mr Lindsey stared at Rita.

She said, "I want some names, Mr Lindsey. The individuals here and in India who are planning this with you. Bogus student visas for fake degrees. For a long time, you've been getting away with it. But now one of your overseas students is dead. The game is up."

Mr Lindsey looked like he was slowly decomposing. Beads of sweat poured down his face, and his collar was damp. His glasses had slipped down his nose. The left eye remained in the same desolate lower left corner, as if slumped in defeat.

His voice seemed to be dragged from a dungeon inside his chest. "That letter is fake. Someone has been impersonating me," he rasped.

"And someone also gave the Indian college false information, claiming you offer a degree course here. Is that correct?"

Mr Lindsey could barely nod.

"And who is that someone?" Richard asked.

"I don't know," Mr Lindsey said in a hoarse voice.

"How long has this been going on?" Rita asked. "These young men and women are ripped from their homes under false pretences, and then they work in the restaurants, don't they? Is it the restaurant owner who pays you for this?"

The principal licked his lips again. "I want a solicitor."

"Was it Yosef Musa? The man who owns the Taj Mahal, among other restaurants?"

Mr Lindsey wiped his forehead with the sleeve of his shirt. "No comment."

"You'll be charged as an accessory to murder," Rita said softly. "That carries a far longer jail sentence than faking documents. Is that what you want, Mr Lindsey? Think about your family. You have two boys at university, don't you?"

Mr Lindsey closed his eyes and passed a hand over his face. His words were a whisper.

"I want a solicitor."

CHAPTER 24

The Major Incident Room, or MIR, was full to the brim. Three uniformed units, Scene of Crime, the Financial Crime Unit, the researchers, and Rita's team were present. So was Nicola Perkins, seated in the front row. Rita faced the assembled officers, standing in front of the projector that beamed Anika's face onto the wall.

"So far, we have strong suspicions of a criminal network at play, which is luring women from South Asian countries to England and then forcing them to work in menial jobs in restaurants, and potentially as sex workers. Our victim was one of the women affected, but there are more."

Rita flicked a button on the remote, and the murder scene on South Beach appeared. "The MO suggests a ritual killing. We have a prime suspect in custody now—Martin Keane. The victim saw him on the day of her death."

"Have you charged him yet?" Nicola asked from the front row.

Rita felt annoyed. Charging someone was only possible when there was ironclad evidence that would stand up in court. Nicola knew that perfectly well, but this was one of her ways to keep Rita under pressure.

"I wish I could click my fingers and create a successful prosecution for the CPS."

Rita's comments drew muted laughter, and she saw Nicola's lips pinch with anger. *Good*, she thought to herself.

"Martin Keane is a known criminal, and he has a history of violence. However, he has never been charged with this type of ritual killing. In fact, a murder with this MO has not occurred in Scarborough before. However, we now have a cold case, is that correct?"

Rita pointed at Rizwan, who stood up to face the room.

"Three years ago, an unidentified female was discovered in the hills near Rosedale. The woman was IC1, and she had been strangled to death and left half-buried up to the waist. She was never identified, and her case was never resolved."

Rizwan sat down. Rita flicked another button, and the cold case photo of the woman found in the hills came up. She was Caucasian, her skin bone white from the lack of blood. Another image showed her buried to the waist in a remote corner of the Rosedale hills.

"This woman was killed using the same MO and preserved in the same way. Her body was discovered by a dog walker. We suspect that the killer is the same. Whether that person is Martin Keane or not, we don't know. What we do know is that Martin still lived in Barrowcliff at that time."

A hand went up, and Rita pointed at Steve Bennett, the uniforms inspector.

Steve said, "We visited the iron ore mines at Rosedale. The victim had iron ore under her nails and on her shoes. If she had been kept there, we didn't find any evidence of it. But it might be that the cold case victim also discovered in Rosedale is not a coincidence."

"Indeed," Rita agreed. "Thank you for checking out the mines at Rosedale. Did you visit the cold case crime scene as well?"

"We did not, but the map shows it's two miles from the iron ore mines."

Rizwan raised a hand. "I've got the forensics report here. That unidentified victim also had iron ore particles under her nails and on her clothes."

"That suggests those mines were used by this killer to either keep his victims or kill them there and later move them." She raised a hand. "Pure conjecture on my part, but the facts seem to suggest it. Can we please treat the mines as a crime scene? Shola?" Rita raised her voice slightly.

"I'm here," Shola said from the third row. She was sitting next to her assistants, Henry and Emily.

"Can you please visit the Rosedale mines and see if there's anything of interest? Thank you. Now, please tell us what you discovered in the victim's house in Barrowcliff."

Shola had updated Rita before the meeting began, but Rita wanted the other officers to be aware of the findings.

Shola said, "We found the victim's DNA and fingerprints everywhere in the house. The other DNA and prints will now be matched to the suspects—Martin, in particular."

"And we took DNA swabs from Mr Lindsey and the restaurant manager, Sachin Agarwal," Rita said. "Both of them are also suspects. We're still looking for the bearded man called Rafik and Yosef Musa."

Shola continued. "The bed mattresses in the victim's house had semen stains. We also found semen on the floor. DNA swabs have been taken. There are no matches so far, but we will keep looking."

"Thank you, Shola," Rita said. She showed another screen where she had written the names of the suspects. Next to each name, the suspects' photos were displayed.

"Yosef Musa doesn't have a police record. We don't know Rafik's last name yet. Gary Faulkes drove the car that picked up Anika on Saturday night, 4th October. Mr Faulkes does have a record—he was arrested last year for narcotics possession. But we haven't apprehended him yet."

Rita looked towards Inspector Bennett again. "Has the car shown up on ANPR? It's important we find the car and the driver ASAP."

Richard spoke up from the front row, where he was sitting next to Rizwan. "Especially since the same car was seen outside the victim's house. It was driven then, according to witness reports, by a man whose description matches Rafik. The car was seen dropping the victim and two other women off and later picking them up."

"Yes, that's correct," Steve responded. "My team conducted the door-to-door, and that was what the neighbours suggested. Can we please have the car on the screen?"

Rita nodded and flicked through the buttons. A brown sedan appeared with 2015 registration plates. She zoomed in on the plates and encouraged everyone to make a note. Pens scratched paper in the silence, and some people took photos.

"I know we have ANPR fitted to the uniformed unit cars and cameras, but it's good to keep an eye out. We still don't know how Anika travelled to the crime scene. She wouldn't have walked from Barrowcliff to South Beach—it was a dark and cold night. Did this car give her a lift? Did it stick to the CCTV dark spots when it drove? It's possible."

Shola raised a hand again and stood. "We also found a phone on the beach. It was washed up in the waves. My colleague, Emily, found it this morning. The phone has Anika's fingerprints and DNA on it. We're looking at it in the lab now. We should have a call log from it soon."

"Thank you, Shola," Rita smiled. "That's a real breakthrough, and I hope we can make more connections from the call list."

Rita took a step closer to the officers. "But most importantly, I think we now have evidence of a network that is essentially trafficking women from India, and maybe other parts of the world, into the UK. I think Mr Lindsey was a key part of this, but we still don't know who the mastermind was."

Nicola spoke again. "But whoever killed Anika put a spanner in their works, correct? If we suspect a human trafficking network, why would they kill one of their victims in such a public manner? They would do the opposite and try to hide their victims."

"Exactly," Rita said, glad Nicola was talking sense for once. "It's likely we have two angles here. We have a killer with the same MO as the cold case from three years ago, and we have the trafficking network. I don't think they're interlinked, as DS Perkins just said—why would the trafficking network publicise their victims by leaving their body on South Beach? They're abusing their victims to make money. It doesn't make sense."

Nicola said, "Is the Modern Slavery Unit involved?"

"Yes," Rita said. It was unusual for Nicola to agree with her investigative methods, but she wasn't complaining. It made her life a lot easier.

"Inspector James Harper will be here from Leeds in an hour. I'm hoping he can shed more light on the likes of Rafik and potentially Yosef Musa."

CHAPTER 25

Yosef Musa was pacing the living room of his flat. He could see himself in the mirror. He was in his late fifties now, but his salt-and-pepper hair was still voluminous and swept back with gel. He had a sharp nose and large, expressive dark eyes. He had looked after himself over the years. As the owner of a restaurant chain, he had to keep up some appearances when he visited his establishments. They were dotted across the North East—Leeds, York, Hull, Bridlington, and Scarborough.

"Calm down," he said. "This attitude is not going to help."

Daniel Lindsey's voice was quivering like a reed in a storm. "Calm down? Are you joking? It's not you who faces total catastrophe. You told me the police would never find out."

Yosef sighed. "I told you to keep your nose clean. Why did you advertise the courses as degrees?"

"Because you wanted more students! Isn't that right?"

"I didn't tell you to lie to our Indian counterparts, did I? All it took was an internet search. That was a dumb move, Daniel."

"Shut up," Lindsey ground back through clenched teeth. "I did what you asked. That's the end of it. Now you need to get the police off my back. They're going to charge me with accessory to murder, for heaven's sake! Never mind losing my reputation—at this rate, I'm going to end up in jail."

"They're just trying to scare you. They think they can bully you into giving them as much information as they need." Musa frowned. "You didn't tell them anything, did you?"

"No. When they threatened me, I told them I wanted a solicitor. After that, they left me alone."

"And they didn't arrest you. There you go. Just stick to that routine."

"For how long? I have a feeling they know about your operation. Don't ask me how. I don't know what the police know, either. But Anika's death has changed everything." Lindsey took a deep breath. "I don't want to do this anymore."

Yosef was quiet for a while. He was upstairs in his duplex flat, and he could hear his son playing downstairs. He shut the door and locked it.

"What do you mean?"

"You heard me. I'm done. Find another college and principal to do your dirty work."

"This storm will pass, okay? You just need to lie low for a while. The police won't go to the media about you. They're worried about getting sued."

Lindsey bit down on each word. "They have my bloody signature on that letter you made me sign. How will I sue them? Yes, I've told them it's a fake letter and not my signature, blah blah. They're not buying it." Lindsey stopped, breathing heavily. "Look, my cover's blown, alright? I can't do this anymore."

"We'll get you a new identity. Some forged qualifications. Get references for you. It can all be done for a price. You need to keep doing your job."

Lindsey was silent for a few seconds. "That sounds like a threat to me."

Yosef spoke quietly. "This door only opens from the inside. You can't just step out and leave. You knew that when you signed up."

Lindsey didn't speak. Yosef continued. "You needed the money, and we helped you. Now you need to carry on with your work. We have new clients in India, Pakistan, Bangladesh. Poland and Lithuania—Bulgaria is also becoming active again."

"You're not hearing me. I'm done."

A niggle of doubt was now assailing Yosef. Lindsey wasn't the only college principal in his pay. They had a network of them. If Lindsey's case got media publicity, then there might be a domino effect with their other players.

Could Lindsey do a deal with the police to keep his anonymity? That could be a disaster. Yosef had got this far in life by eliminating any sign of an impending disaster.

"Your son Brian has his second-semester exams at Durham University, doesn't he? How's his new flat coming along?"

Lindsey breathed heavily down the phone. "You wouldn't dare."

"Don't try me," Yosef said softly. "If you speak to the cops, or if you try to cut a deal with them, we will know. This won't end well for your family."

Yosef also knew he couldn't push Lindsey too far. He might crack, and then it was game over. He took a conciliatory tone.

"Look, just take some leave, stay at home, and wait for this to blow over. It will, I promise you. We'll take care of it."

Yosef hung up. He looked outside the window, at the houses opposite, and the church steeple rising in the distance. Then he called another number, one he stored in this burner phone.

"It's me," Yosef said.

"Have the detectives been to see you?" the male voice asked.

"Not as yet. But I think they will. They've been to the restaurant and spoken to Sachin. They also spoke to Priya, one of the girls. I don't think she told them anything. I watched the CCTV. The detective didn't give Priya a card, or not that I could see. She was close to Anika. We need to keep an eye on her."

"Yes, we do. The lead detective's name is Rita Gupta, correct?"

"Yes, she's the one who went to the restaurant and also saw Lindsey, with her sergeant—Richard something."

"I'll make enquiries. We might have to control this Rita Gupta. She's getting too big for her boots."

Yosef nodded. "I think so too."

CHAPTER 26

Rita was at Roshni Community Centre. She went on her own because she wanted to speak to the women by herself. Poonam wasn't at the front desk, but she was shown to Poonam's office. Rita knocked on the door, and when she heard a muffled voice, she entered. Poonam was with another woman, who looked like a client. She had a child with her, a boy no more than ten years old.

"Sorry to interrupt," Rita said. "But can I please have a word?"

Poonam spoke to the woman in a low voice, and the woman rose. The boy held onto his mother's hand, looking at Rita curiously as he walked past her.

"Thanks for seeing me," Rita said, taking a seat. "We went to the restaurant where Anika worked. Do you know a woman called Priya Malhotra? She was friends with Anika."

"Hang on," Poonam said. She clicked on her keyboard and looked at her screen. Then she shook her head. "No one with that name has registered with us. It doesn't ring a bell with me, anyway."

"Anika came here to ask for help. She already had a job, but she hated it. We now suspect a human trafficking ring at work. She was abused and scared when she came to see you." Rita paused. "Are you sure she didn't tell you anything else?"

Poonam frowned. "Apart from what I've told you so far? No."

"She did have a phone. We found it today, washed up on the beach."

Poonam's eyebrows rose as the corners of her mouth relaxed. "Oh. She didn't tell us that. She didn't even mention a passport."

"The passport might've been taken from her. But you're certain she didn't give you a phone number or try to call you?"

Poonam's eyes narrowed. "What are you trying to say, Inspector? That I lied to you? That in secret, Anika was trying to stay in touch with me, but I didn't tell you?"

"I'm not here to make accusations, Poonam. In your line of work, I know it can get personal sometimes. You help people out because…" Rita raised the tips of her shoulders, making it clear she wasn't here to be judgemental.

Poonam seemed to relax. She sat back in her chair. "No, Anika didn't stay in touch with me. I wish she had, to be honest. I could see she was scared. To be honest, I thought she might be involved in something dodgy. I did think she might be an illegal immigrant here. I didn't tell you that when I saw you, I'm sorry. But I guess you picked up on that, didn't you?"

"Yes. We now think there's a human trafficking network operating here. It could be a branch of a bigger operation across the North East."

Rita watched Poonam. She didn't think the woman was lying. The call log from Anika's phone would show Poonam's number if she was lying.

"Anika worked at the Taj Mahal restaurant. Have you heard of it?"

Poonam pressed her lips together. "Yes, but not good things. Hang on, our director, Paul, knows more. Shall I get him?"

"Yes, please."

Poonam returned shortly with Paul Manning. He was dressed in a khaki vest with large brown buttons, blue jeans with frayed edges, and leather slippers. He looked more like a hippie or surfer dude than the owner and manager. His kind eyes crinkled at the corners.

"How are things, Inspector? Any closer to finding out what happened to Anika?"

"We have made significant strides, yes. We found her phone, for instance. She wanted to hide that from everyone, including yourselves, obviously."

Paul nodded without speaking, looking thoughtful. "Poonam was saying Anika worked at the Taj Mahal restaurant, is that correct?"

"Yes, and so does her friend, Priya. I'm worried about her, to be honest."

Paul pulled up a chair and sat down. "Between you and me, Inspector, the Taj Mahal has always had a reputation. Their waiters have been our clients before, but now I think they're scared to admit it. We suspect there might be something dodgy going on there, but no one speaks up."

"What have you heard, specifically?" Rita also looked at Poonam, who was staring at them across the table.

"Just whispers, you understand. They take the female waitresses out of the restaurant at night and use them as ladies of the night. Sometimes also to carry things, like drugs."

"Who told you this?"

Poonam answered. "Some of the women who work there. But they were very scared. They've been browbeaten into submission. They're told their families will suffer if they reveal anything."

Paul said, "The owner is a man called Yosef Musa. He owns a number of restaurants across the region." He dropped his voice. "I know where he lives."

"How is that?" Rita was interested.

"Well, it's a long story, but the short version is, he's also from Bradford. Nice guy, actually. Charismatic. We started off in Bradford, as you will recall. His office was close to ours, and I asked him one day how to expand and so on. He was very helpful, although our business is public tax-funded charity work, so very different. Nevertheless, he was an interesting man back then."

Rita got the impression Paul was being polite and not really speaking his mind.

"Did you trust him?" she prodded.

Paul smiled. "He was a slick businessman. The type who'll do anything to get ahead in life. Know what I mean?"

"I do." She took her leather notebook out. "Where in Bradford does he live?"

Rita took a cab back from Roshni's office near the town centre, although she could've walked. She wanted to get back as soon as possible, as Richard had called to say Inspector James Harper from the Modern Slavery Unit had turned up. Rita opened the office door to find him speaking to Rizwan and Richard. He stood and shook hands with Rita.

"Call me James, please. Nice to meet you."

A good-looking man, Rita noted. Dark brown, short-cut hair, olive-green eyes that glinted with a hint of amusement, and a sharp nose that tapered into firm, well-set lips.

"Heard good things about you, DI Gupta. You've made quite the impression on the North Yorkshire Police force. The child abduction case was covered in the papers, and your name was mentioned."

"It was nothing," Rita smiled and waved a hand. When she thought of the last case, her mind lingered on Maggie. She hadn't called her and made a point to do so when she went home tonight.

James pointed at the whiteboard where Rita had written the names of the suspects and Anika. Rizwan had added his colour-coded lines—black, blue, and purple—connecting the dots. He had even put Anika's name in a circle and drawn spokes with the suspects' names.

"I see you've got the names of Yosef and Rafik in there," James said. "Those two men have been on our radar for a while. But they have a group in India who's helping them. They have operations in all of the major Indian towns, closer to the villages. That's where the poorer people live, with low levels of education. Prime hunting ground for human traffickers."

"Who else do you suspect?" Rita asked.

Harper opened his briefcase and took out a folder and a map. From the folder, he took out photos of a few men, along with information on them. He spread the map on Rita's desk. Red circles had been drawn over the cities of Manchester, Liverpool, Leeds, and Hull.

"Manchester International Airport is the main transport hub, as it has regular flights from the main cities in India and Pakistan. From there, the victims are taken by car to their destinations. It's rare for them to come this far, to be honest. But we have made several arrests in Manchester and Leeds recently. Our informers are active on the streets. Both cities, and Sheffield, have a large British Asian community, and they have helped immensely."

"There's a community centre here called Roshni. Their director, Paul Manning, apparently knows Yosef Musa from back when he worked in Bradford."

"He does?" Harper looked interested.

"Yes. And I've got Musa's address in Bradford. I'm going to pay him a visit." Rita turned to Rizwan. "Can you please get hold of West Yorkshire Police in Bradford? Alert them about Yosef. I want to see him myself."

"I think you'll find the Bradford police are aware of him already," Harper said. "I know the DI in one of the city branches. His name's Mansoor Ahmed. Shall I put you in touch?"

Rita smiled at him. "That would be amazing, thank you."

Harper made the call and then hung up. "He'll call you back to set the meeting up."

"That's great." Rita could see Harper was an experienced inspector, and she was glad he had joined the team. She looked down at the map on her desk, and then at the photos of Yosef and Rafik. She noted Rafik matched the description – a lean face, light beard, and she could just make out a scar on the left cheek, hidden by his beard.

"What's Rafik's full name?"

Harper handed her the one-page information sheet with Rafik's photo on it. His name was Rafik Khan, and he had multiple PCNs for GBH and assault and had served two sentences for assault and battery.

Rita said, "At the Taj Mahal restaurant, there's a manager called Sachin Agarwal. He's short, pot-bellied, with acne scars on his face. Clean-shaven. IC3."

Harper narrowed his eyes. "That sounds familiar."

Richard said, "I looked up Sachin's details from the Home Office. He flies to India often. He returned from New Delhi six weeks ago. That's his fifth trip this year. He doesn't have any PCNs, but he does have a business in India, which has a branch in Leicester. He sells English language books and courses, which he sells in India and other countries."

"And works here as a restaurant manager? That doesn't make sense," Rizwan said. "I wonder if the restaurant is really a front for something else?"

"I think it is a restaurant," Richard said. "Remember our witness who spotted Anika there? Taj Mahal has customers. Sachin could have a side business."

"Yes, Sachin could be running multiple businesses on the side," Rita said. "He just helps out at the Taj, which is part of Yosef Musa's restaurant chain." She thought of Sam, Jack's friend. Maybe she needed to contact him again.

Harper said, "A man with the same description as Sachin has been on our radar for a while. We need to investigate him. I can allocate resources for surveillance. Would you like me to do that?"

"Yes, please," Rita said.

"OK. Send me his details and I'll see what I can do."

Rita said, "I need to interview Martin Keane now. He was probably the last person to see Anika alive."

Richard spoke to Harper. "What about Martin Keane and Gary Faulks? Have they been on your radar?"

Harper wanted to see their photos and PCN details. Then he nodded slowly. "No, I don't think so. I'll ask my head office and get more info for you."

Rita pointed at Richard. "Let's go and meet Mr Keane."

CHAPTER 27

Martin Keane sat up straighter when Rita entered. He wore a brown T-shirt, and he had a week's stubble on his cheeks. He was wide-shouldered but slim. His hands rested on the table, fingernails stained yellow with tobacco. Hate glittered in his eyes, and his jaws ground together as Rita and Richard took seats opposite him.

The interview room had a green lino floor, and the chair and table legs were screwed to the floor. A round clock ticked on the wall behind Martin. There was a drinks machine in the corner, beneath a viewing box that was a rectangular, dark window. Rita suspected Nicola Perkins was watching from the viewing chamber. It would be nice of Nicola to tell Rita that, as her previous bosses used to. But Rita knew Nicola didn't care if Rita knew or not.

Martin had a solicitor, a man in a blue suit. He wore glasses and had a balding head, despite being no more than in his thirties. Rita hadn't seen him before, but Rizwan had informed her he was Dean Curchod, the duty solicitor.

Rita spoke to Dean first. "We can conduct this interview informally to get more information from your client. If he cooperates, then we might be able to release him without charge. Or we can record our discussion. How would you like to proceed?"

Dean had a hushed discussion with Martin, who shook his head vehemently. Rita knew the answer before Dean cleared his throat.

"My client wishes me to represent him. Please record this."

Rita nodded. Sometimes people talked more if the interview was not recorded, as then nothing could be used in court against them. But Martin clearly knew the game was up. He didn't want to talk, full stop.

Richard spoke into the machine and introduced everyone. Rita fixed Martin with a stare.

"Tell us how you know Anika Joshi."

"No comment."

Rita had expected nothing else. She signalled to Richard, who produced printouts of the CCTV images. Rita pushed the photos across the desk. They showed Martin and Anika arguing inside the pub and walking on the road. There was also an image of Anika standing outside Martin's house.

Rita pointed at the last image. "Showing Evidence 1A from Folder B. That is your front door, is that correct?"

Martin seemed to have lost the power of speech. He tried hard to remain impassive, an almost bored expression on his face, but it was forced. His breathing was faster, and his hands moved under the table.

"Can you please answer the question?"

Martin looked at his lawyer, who nodded. Martin said, "Yes, that's my house."

Richard produced a tablet device from his briefcase and turned it to the CCTV coverage. The video showed Martin arguing with Anika.

"And that's you in the Crown and Sceptre pub, arguing with the victim?"

Dean intervened. "I'm sorry, Inspector Gupta, but you have no proof that they were arguing. Also, apart from a physical similarity, there is no conclusive proof that the woman in that photo was the victim."

Rita gave him a withering look. "Facial recognition software will identify her, and it is clear to anyone involved in the case that the woman on the screen is Anika Joshi, the victim. You have not been involved in the case, have you, Mr Curchod?"

Dean seemed to shrink under Rita's glare. He cleared his throat. "Nevertheless, we need proof—"

"We have proof," Richard spoke up. "Your client is well aware of who that woman is, otherwise he would not be arguing with her."

Rita hadn't moved her eyes away from Martin. "Now can you please answer the question? That is you, with the victim, in the pub?"

Martin had recovered some of his composure. He didn't break eye contact with Rita. "Yes."

Rita said, "It's clear that you were having an argument with the victim. This occurred on Friday, 3rd October, at 20:30 hours. What were you discussing?"

"One of her friends was in some trouble, and she wanted to talk about that." He shrugged, feigning nonchalance. "That's all it was."

"So you knew her well?"

"I had met her a couple of times in the pub, like you do. Did I know her well? No, can't say that, like."

His accent was the typical North Yorkshire brogue. He was used to these parts, and to this police station, where he had been interviewed before. He was a seasoned operator, but he wasn't fooling Rita or Richard.

"If you didn't know her well, why was she at your house on the morning of the day she died?"

Rita put emphasis on the last word. She saw it hit home, but Martin took it well. He shrugged again.

"She came to tell me her friend was all right and thanked me."

Richard was busy looking at the CCTV footage on the tablet device. "She went inside and didn't leave for one hour. It doesn't take that long to say thank you, does it?"

"She had a cuppa, like, you know. That was all."

"A cuppa for one hour?" Rita asked in a scathing tone. "Or were you doing something else?"

Martin said nothing, yet his eyes were alive with a strange light, and he didn't avert them from Rita's. She sensed an opening.

"Mr Keane, were you in a relationship with Anika Joshi? Were you romantically involved with her?"

"No comment," Martin drawled slowly.

Dean cleared his throat. "DI Gupta, this is highly speculative and has no part to play in this case. The victim could have met with any number of people on the day of her death. My client meeting her was merely a coincidence."

Rita ignored him and stared back at Martin. His jaws flexed, and the light dulled in his eyes as he shifted in his seat. He looked away.

"Tell us what happened to Anika, Mr Keane," Rita said softly. "You cared for her, didn't you? We only argue and quarrel with the people we care about."

Martin made a bored look appear on his face again, but he was acting. He bent his lips downward.

"Nope, she was just a friend, that's all. Nowt else."

"And yet she remained in your house for more than an hour. Just drinking tea," Rita said.

"No comment."

Rita decided to try a different angle. "Anika was also seen with a bearded, Asian man of Indian or Pakistani origin. We have reason to believe she was kept in virtual slavery by this man and his associates. Did she talk to you about that?"

Martin stiffened slightly, then a shadow passed over his face. "No comment."

"We believe Anika was trafficked from India. She was held against her will and used in forced labour as well as a sex worker. And she wasn't the only one." The disturbance was now clear on Martin's face, like a stone rippling the surface of a still, deep pond.

Rita leaned forward. "You knew about that, didn't you, Martin?"

His jaws flexed once. Rita asked, "Can you please answer the question?"

"No comment."

"You took a fancy to her. You wanted her for yourself. But maybe she wanted you to fight for her. Take her away from the men who had snatched her, kept her captive. But you didn't want that fight, did you?"

Martin glared at Rita and said nothing. She continued. "You had enough trouble on your plate after your fight with the bikers. They were stepping on your toes, weren't they? Coming onto your turf?"

Martin's eyes narrowed for an instant as if wondering where Rita got that information from.

She said, "So you didn't want to protect Anika. You didn't want a showdown with the trafficking gang. But Anika kept asking you, and maybe she said she was going to the police."

Rita stopped, ensuring she had Martin's attention. His eyebrows were lowered now, and a muscle ticked in his forehead.

"If Anika came to us, you had a problem. So, you decided to eliminate her. On Monday, 6th October, you planned to meet her on South Beach."

"No," Martin breathed in a low voice, his jaws clenched tight. A wave of scarlet was spreading up his neck.

"You tried to reason with her, but she wouldn't listen. In a moment of fury, you grabbed her by the neck. You couldn't control yourself. You squeezed her neck until she stopped breathing, her eyes staring at you—"

"No!" Martin roared, rising from his seat. He thrust himself backwards against the wall, and the chair would've toppled over if it wasn't nailed to the floor. His cheeks were inflamed, and deep breaths heaved in his chest.

"I didn't do that."

Rita sat still, as if nothing had happened. "You felt bad, so you half covered her in sand. You came back later, in a blue van, opposite the Royal Hotel."

"No!" Martin shouted again. "None of this is true." Sweat congealed on his forehead. He shot a wild look at his solicitor. Dean turned to Rita, shaking his head.

"DI Gupta. Has this not gone far enough?"

Rita cut her eyes at him. "If your client is not guilty, why is he acting so emotionally? He's aware of what he's done. The guilt is eating him from inside. Isn't that right?" She looked back at Martin.

"No." Martin's face twisted in sudden pain. Sorrow now lay heavy on his shoulders, pressing him down. He looked at the floor.

"I loved her. I'd never kill her."

"Then tell us what happened to her. Who did this to Anika?"

Martin remained where he was, slumped against the wall. "It's like you said. She was brought here by those men. They took her passport when she got here. I met her first when one of the kids at the pub told me she was looking for a phone. I sold her one, and we got talking."

Rita glanced at Richard. That would be the phone they had just discovered on the beach.

"What did she tell you?"

"Just what I said." Martin lifted his head. There was a lost, vacant look in his eyes now. He seemed to stare through Rita, as if his mind was miles away.

"They kept her in that house. Yes, she was a prostitute and worked in that restaurant. I can't remember the name now. She hated the blokes who ran the place."

"Any names?" Richard asked.

Martin nodded. "Aye. There was a guy called Rafik. I've seen him around as well, in Barrowcliff and also in town. He's new to these parts. Not seen him before the last six months or so."

Rita pointed at the chair. "Sit down." She glanced at Richard, who understood. He got up and got a plastic cup of water from the drinks machine. Martin took a sip, and when he put the cup down, his hand trembled.

Rita said, "Did Anika mention anyone else?"

"The man who ran the restaurant. Yosie or summat, I can't remember."

"Yosef Musa."

"That's the one."

"Did you ever meet him? Or Rafik?"

"I've seen Rafik around, but not to say hello, or owt. Didn't know him. Or Musa." Martin looked at Rita. He was different now, a dull, defeated glaze in his eyes. "Another guy drove them around. Gary, his name is. I've seen Gary around. He did some jobs for me, back in the day. Transporting stuff."

"Gary Faulks?"

"Yes, that's him."

Rita nodded, happy to let Martin's past slide for now. "Did Gary have a blue van? Or did he ever go by the name of Andy Stetson?"

Martin frowned. "No. You mentioned a blue van before. I don't know owt about that."

Rita believed him this time. "Okay."

"She mentioned another person. She didn't know who it was. The men spoke to him on the phone. The men asked him what to do. He gave them orders."

Next to Rita, Richard stirred. She felt the snap of urgency as well. "Who was he? Did they mention a name?"

Martin shook his head. "Anika never got to know. But the men seemed scared of him. They called him boss. That's all she knew."

CHAPTER 28

Rita came out of the interview room and was walking past the viewing room when she saw the door ajar and heard voices inside. She knocked and looked in to find Nicola Perkins, as she had suspected. James Harper was with her as well, which surprised her. He hurried over to Rita.

"My boss asked me to report to DS Perkins as well." His eyes searched her face, judging her reaction. Rita wasn't happy about it, but she couldn't blame Harper. It made sense that his boss would want to clear Harper's presence here with Nicola.

"I hope you don't mind," he said, and behind his handsome features, she sensed a little anxiety.

"It's fine," she said, relaxing. She caught Nicola listening to their conversation. She went inside the room, telling Richard to go upstairs.

"What did you think of Martin's confession?" Rita asked Nicola and Harper.

"Well done on breaking him down," Harper smiled. "That was good. You've done this before, eh?"

"Once or twice," Rita said, looking askance at Nicola, who was observing coldly, arms folded across her chest. She looked like a little, pint-sized Russian doll, devoid of any expression.

"There's someone above the gang, controlling everything," Rita said. "He's within reach of Rafik, Yosef and the others. We need to find him."

"Yes," Harper nodded. "What's the plan of action?"

Rita was glad that he was acknowledging her role as the SIO. Which she was, of course. Normally, with other male Inspectors called in to help, she would have to stamp her authority, as they often thought they could call the shots. Harper had shown his maturity by deferring to her, and she liked that.

"Our priority has to be to get Yosef. I think he's more senior to Rafik. Did you speak to your colleague in Bradford?"

"DI Mansoor Ahmed? Or Mans, as I call him. No, he wasn't in his office, but I left word for him. However, we know where Yosef's office might be, right? You found out from that guy in the community centre."

"Paul Manning told us, yes. I want to head over to Bradford, but we need to apprehend Rafik here as well. For that, I can leave Richard and Rizwan in charge." She glanced at Nicola. "Is that alright, guv?"

"All I want is a suspect. We have to do a press conference soon, and I need some answers." Nicola pointed at the now-empty interview room. "Are you going to charge him?"

"I don't think he did it," Rita said. "The trafficking gang had more to gain from silencing Anika."

"Then why would they leave her in a public place that got all the attention?"

"I'm not sure, but I think if we dismantle the criminal network that got Anika here, we'll get our answer to that."

"I hope you do soon, Rita. Chief Constable Grant rang me this morning. I told him we have a suspect in custody, but now it seems you have to let him go. He won't be pleased, I can assure you."

"We're trying our best, ma'am, as you can see. We should have another suspect in custody soon."

"See that happens by the end of today," Nicola said. She lifted her chin and walked out of the room like she was marching to a military band.

"She always like this?" Harper whispered after she'd gone.

"I think she just really likes me," Rita scoffed. "You just have to put up with her. Anyway, let's get cracking."

They came out of the custody chambers, where Martin would be held for twenty-four hours. As they went up the stairs, Rita asked Harper if he would go to Bradford with her.

"Sorry, I can't. My boss wants me back in Leeds for another case. I'll catch up with you tomorrow if that's okay?"

"No worries. Thanks for your help so far."

"Call me anytime," Harper said, smiling with his faultless white teeth. "Do you want me to call DI Mansoor Ahmed and let him know that you'll be going over?"

"Yes, please, thank you."

Rita said goodbye and hurried over to the office. Rizwan and Richard were standing in front of the map.

Rizwan turned as Rita entered, and he looked animated. "The DNA report came back. The sperm found inside Anika is a positive match with Martin. His fingerprints are on her clothes as well, and also in her house."

"But not on her skin," Richard added.

"Hmm," Rita replied, sipping a glass of water. "Perhaps we hold Martin till tomorrow, see if he remembers owt else."

"Owt? You sound Yorkshire, guv," Rizwan smiled, as did Richard.

"I was born here, or have you forgotten? I lived here before you did." Rita grinned, stretching her arms and yawning. "Any news of the call log from Anika's phone?"

"Yes." Rizwan sat down at his desk and shook out an A4 paper from the mess. "We don't recognise most of the numbers. But Martin Keane features there. So does the FETC – just the switchboard, mind. She also tried to call India several times, but from the call duration of a few seconds, looks like she didn't have enough credit on her phone."

"The phone that Martin gave her," Rita said. "Possibly a pay-as-you-go burner phone. Keep cross-checking all the numbers. We must have numbers for the suspects?"

"Checked against those. Nowt against Yosef or Rafik. She did call one number a few times over the weeks before her death, and on the day. I'll keep trying to track it, but it's a needle in a haystack."

"Speak to Traffic and see if you can triangulate the locations." Rita glanced at her watch. It was past 1 pm. "Shall we get some lunch? Then I want to head to Bradford. I want you two to stay here and catch Rafik, if you can."

They walked to the canteen, and Rita sat down with them. Her mind was churning, convolutions appearing like bends in the road as she moved in a fast car.

"Did Priya get back to us? The waitress at the Taj Mahal restaurant."

"Not as yet," Rizwan said.

"Let's find out where she lives. She knew Anika, she should be able to help us more." She looked at Rizwan. "Can you please head down to the restaurant and see if you can get hold of her?"

"No worries, guv."

They went back to the office, and Rita had one job she couldn't delay any longer. It was half past two in the afternoon now, and it would be around 7 pm in India. But she had to make the call. Rizwan called out the number from his phone while she dialled.

A man answered the phone. "Hello? Who is this?"

"What's your name, please?"

"Anish Joshi. Who are you?" His name sounded similar to Anika's, and Rita wondered if he was her brother.

"My name is DI Rita Gupta of North Yorkshire Police in England. I am calling about Anika Joshi. Is she related to you?"

There was silence on the other line. Then the man spoke louder and faster. "Anika? Yes, she's my sister. You know where she is?"

"Yes. Do you know when she left India?"

"Where is she? How is Anika?"

Rita could now hear a woman's voice, and then a bubble of other voices. The family was joining in, eager to hear news of their loved one. This was going to be harder than Rita had imagined. Two women were speaking in Hindi, Rita assumed, and Anish was trying his best to answer them. Then he came on the line.

"Where is Anika? Is she in trouble?"

Rita closed her eyes. "I'm sorry, Mr Joshi. I've got some bad news. Anika is dead."

The stunned silence at the other end of the line was prolonged. Then the other voices faded, and Rita realised Anish had taken the phone to another room.

"What happened to her?"

Rita described how Anika's body was found on the beach. "I'm so sorry. I know how hard this is for you." She waited. From the sounds on the other end, she knew Anish was unable to control his emotions, and she didn't blame him.

"Who did this to her?" he asked finally.

"To find that out, I need to ask you a few things..."

CHAPTER 29

Rita carried on, having paused to think. "Firstly, how did Anika apply to the Scarborough FETC? Who told her about it?"

"You mean the University of Scarborough? Two men here ran a further education agency that helped students go abroad for their studies. They approached Anika, and she wanted to apply."

"There is no University of Scarborough," Rita said. "Who were these two men? Do you have their names and contact details?"

"Yes. One was called Sunil Seth. The other was Manish something. Hang on, I've got their details here." Rita heard a drawer open and shut. "Manish Singh."

"Did you meet these men? Do you know what they're like?"

"Yes, I met them once. Sunil is short, with a pot belly. He's got pox marks on his face. Manish is taller and younger, slimmer." He stopped. "Have you seen them in the UK?"

"No, we haven't, but we will keep a look out."

Anish cursed down the line, his emotions taking over again. "I knew this was a bad idea. I told my parents, but they were keen on Anika achieving her ambition of becoming a fashion designer. Oh God."

"We will get to the bottom of this, Mr Joshi. Do you know if this education agency is still working?"

"No. We didn't hear from Anika after she left, so we called them. But their office was closed down, there was no sign on the wall, and the other shopkeepers had no idea where they went. It was called New Horizons."

Rita wondered if India had a central database of all companies where the directors had to register and so on. She had no idea. But she could get in touch with the IPA, or the Indian Police Association. Many years ago, a murderer in London had escaped to India, and she had sought the help of the Indian police to bring him to justice.

"Thank you for your help. I know this is hard for you, and believe me, we will do absolutely everything to find out what happened to Anika."

Anish couldn't speak. Rita heard the women's voices again. They had come into Anish's room, maybe, and wanted answers. Rita's heart broke when she thought of what the family would go through now. They wouldn't have any closure, only empty questions. Their grief was palpable, even across the frail phone line and thousands of miles of distance.

"Find out who did this to my sister," Anish's voice choked with grief. "Please."

"I will," Rita said, her jaws flexing. "I promise you, I will."

Rita took the train to Bradford and then a cab to the police station in Shipley, a suburb of Bradford. Shipley had a large station, one of West Yorkshire Police's main hubs in the city. The duty sergeant showed her in through the double doors of the waiting room when she presented her warrant card to him. Inspector Ahmed was waiting for her inside the atrium that led into a corridor, accessible through steel double doors. Rita noted the iron grilles in the hallways, reminding her of a prison's interior.

"We had riots in Shipley three years ago," DI Ahmed explained. "The rioters broke in through reception and flooded the nick. Since then, we have compartments in every section."

"I heard about them," Rita remembered. It was reported in the national media as riots in Bradford, but Shipley wasn't mentioned as a location. "Happened all over the city, right?"

"Yes. It started in Jamestown, Leeds, where a young offender died in prison."

"Sorry you had to deal with that. We had our own down in London, back in 2011."

They went to his office, where DI Ahmed showed Rita a folder on Yosef Musa. "He's a clever operator. Runs a number of legitimate businesses, but we suspect he washes money for a number of gangsters by allowing them to invest in his businesses. The restaurant chain is his biggest activity, but he also has supermarkets and nightclubs in Bradford and Leeds."

"Have you suspected him of human trafficking?"

"Whispers have surrounded him in allegations of prostitution and, yes, trafficking. Some victims have spoken out, but they were then paid hush money, we suspect, as they never testified in court against him. He's a canny operator. He likes to portray himself as a leader of the community. Donates to charity and that. But it's all bollocks."

Rita showed Ahmed the address Paul had given her. Ahmed looked through his screen and nodded. "Yes, that's his residential address. I called earlier, but he's busy apparently. Shall we pay him a visit?"

They went in Ahmed's car. The house turned out to be a high-walled mansion in an exclusive residential suburb. Ahmed parked, and they got out. Birds called in the trees, and the grime and traffic of the main drag seemed to have faded in the distance.

"Nice place," Rita said. "I wonder why he needs a house this big if he lives on his own. But I guess he has to park his money somewhere."

"Exactly."

Ahmed rang the bell, but there was no response. The heavy wooden door was firmly closed, and the high walls were covered in ivy. After a few more rings and thumping the door hard, they moved around in opposite directions. The rear of the property opened out into fields and woodlands, separated from the road by a grass verge and a waist-high fence.

They went back and tried the front door again, with the same result. Ahmed rang the house phone, but no one answered.

"He might be away," Rita suggested. "But that's not what your informers said, correct?"

"Yes. He's been seen this morning in this area. He was out walking by himself, talking on the phone. A patrolling uniforms team saw him."

Ahmed rang his team back at the station and was told there had been no more sightings of Yosef since this morning.

"Let's go over the back," Rita suggested. "If he's not in the house, he's probably gone." At the back of her mind, an unease was growing. Yosef was aware he was under watch. She had missed her chance to grab him.

They jogged lightly to the rear of the property, Ahmed carrying a portable ladder which he had stored in the boot of his car. Rita was the first one to vault over the fence, taking the ladder from Ahmed. Getting over the high walls was more of an issue, but Ahmed held the ladder steady while Rita climbed up. She straddled the top, not enjoying the undignified manner of her climb. Luckily, there was a flat roof on a garden room just below the wall. She jumped on it and grunted as she sprained her left ankle. The garden room wasn't big, less than three metres high. She was able to get down easily. She tested her left foot gingerly. It was sore, but she could weight bear.

Ahmed joined her, and they walked up to the wide glass door of the rear conservatory. Behind the conservatory, the red brick mansion rose up to two floors.

The conservatory door was open. Four steps led up to the door. Rita put a gloved hand on the door handle and stopped. The conservatory lounge was wide, and a white Persian carpet was laid on the floor. There was a massive flat-screen TV on the wall and a set of leather sofas opposite. The white carpet was in the middle, but it wasn't white anymore.

It was turning red and black from the blood that seeped out of the skull and mouth of the man lying on it.

Rita cursed and opened the door wider. She looked around and then behind at Ahmed. He had already backed out and circled with a hand, signifying he was going to do a quick recon. He pulled out his radio and spoke into it softly.

Rita went inside, careful not to step on the blood or any other object. She crouched a few feet away from the man's head. It was Yosef Musa. His face had been battered with a blunt object, and it was swollen and deformed, but he was still recognisable. His mouth was open, tongue visible. His hands were bloodied, and the crimson tide had tarnished his green dressing gown.

Rita felt her heart thudding with adrenaline as she stared at him. He was dead as a doorknob.

CHAPTER 30

The terraced house in Eastfield, south of Scarborough, had been converted into two apartments. It was small and dingy, the walls covered in patches of damp. Mould grew in the corners. It was still daylight, but the curtains were drawn. It was dark inside.

Priya lived with the other women in the apartment upstairs. She heard voices outside and pressed her ear to the door. She could hear her friend, Sheila, and another voice she couldn't hear properly.

She opened the door a crack. She saw Sheila's back, but she couldn't see the man's face.

"You want more money?" the man's voice raged. It was Rafik. He slapped her across the back of her head. Sheila cowered, whimpering.

Priya opened the door, and light spilled into the corridor. "Leave her alone," she said.

Rafik snarled, focusing his attention on her.

"What will you do?" He advanced towards Priya. He was a big bloke, and his heavy arms had hit the women countless times. But Priya stood her ground. She had a pretty face, and the man used her in various ways.

"If you hit me, I'll tell the boss," she said.

Rafik stood there, breathing heavily.

Priya watched him, her heart hammering, breath rasping in her lungs. She knew Rafik wouldn't hit her in the face. If she had a bruise, she couldn't be used as a sex worker. Priya was pretty, and the men liked her.

"Get back inside," Rafik snarled. "And be grateful for what you're getting. You stupid bitches."

Sheila shrank away as he walked past her. Rafik reached out a hand and shoved Sheila, pushing her against the wall. Then the door slammed, and they heard him going down the stairs.

Priya hurried over to her, and the two women went inside the apartment. Five of them lived in this tiny place. The other three women were out working for the evening. Sheila was sick, hence she had time off from the gruelling shifts she worked in the restaurant.

Priya worked as a waitress, then at night, servicing the men chosen for her. There was another man called Mak or Makhdoom. There was also Gary and Sachin. Between the three of them, they transported and terrorised the women into submission.

Priya held Sheila's hand as she dried her eyes. Sheila hadn't been in England for long. Only four weeks. She came from a village back in Punjab. Her parents had sent her here on a student visa, thinking she was studying. The truth was very different. The visa turned out to be fake, and the college of higher learning non-existent. The men who got her the visa had taken her passport as soon as she left Manchester Airport. Now, like Priya, she worked as a waitress in another Indian restaurant in town at night and fixed nails in a beauty salon in the daytime. All the businesses were controlled by the gangs.

"Don't ask for money," Priya told her as she flopped down on the bed.

Priya had been here for more than a year. Her smooth face was marked by the hard press of her lips, and the dull, lifeless look in her eyes. She too had learnt the art of not protesting. But she also knew how to stand up for herself.

Sheila opened her palm. Inside rested two twenty-pound notes. "That's for a whole week's work?" Tears budded in her eyes. "I don't have a phone, I don't have a bank card. Never mind my passport. I work like a dog all day. What sort of a life is this?"

She buried her head in her hands and sobbed.

Priya gripped her shoulder. "You'll get used to it. I'm sorry. But there's no other way."

Sheila wiped her eyes. "There must be. I want to get out of here. Please help me."

"You don't think I've tried?" Priya held Sheila's eyes. "I saved up money and took the train. I went to Leeds and ended up homeless. They found me eventually, through one of their contacts. I was thrashed to within an inch of my life. You don't know what they're capable of."

Sheila stared at Priya's vacant, glass-like eyes. They reminded her of a dead person's basilisk stare.

"And that threat of killing your family back home? It's not an idle one." Priya's face twisted in sorrow, and her head dropped.

Sheila clutched her hand and leaned forward to hug her.

Priya sobbed once. "They killed my brother. Then they sent me a photo. In India, no one cares. They paid the police off, and the investigation was dropped."

The women hugged, then Priya separated and dried her eyes. The flat, hard look was back on her face.

"Remember what happened to Anika?"

Sheila nodded slowly. "Who killed her?"

"One of them. I don't know what happened, but it's the kind of thing they would do, to make an example of us."

Sheila stared at Priya, frozen in shock.

"So there's no point. Don't ask for anything. Just survive."

"You call this surviving? Five of us here in this tiny flat. Getting beaten and raped. In the restaurants, the drunk men abuse us. I'd rather be dead."

Priya's face was a mask, and it chilled Sheila. It was as if she barely allowed herself any emotion. Apart from the revelation about her brother, she always kept herself quiet and aloof. Now Sheila knew why.

"I've been there too," Priya whispered. "But taking your own life is not easy."

She stood, walked over to her corner, and sat down on her bed. The men had moved them here on Tuesday from their previous house in Barrowcliff. Priya had learnt of Anika's death from one of the women at Roshni, whom she met in town. Then the police came.

Priya reached inside her jeans pocket and pulled out the card that the detective inspector had left for her. Rita Gupta. She was nice, Priya thought. The men told her not to trust the police, that they would put her in jail for being an illegal immigrant.

But would jail be worse than this?

And if she was in jail, wouldn't the police get her in touch with her family?

There was only one problem. She didn't have a phone. She couldn't use the phone in the restaurant. If she went for a walk, the men told her she'd be watched. If she went inside a phone box, she might get reported. And she hadn't seen a phone box around here. She didn't even know if they existed.

She had to get herself a phone.

Or get in touch with Inspector Rita Gupta, somehow.

And she knew who could help her.

CHAPTER 31

The Night Before

The dingy terraced house was tucked away in the back alleys near Scarborough town. On the ground floor, there was a nail parlour, and the flat above was the main destination. The Watcher had been here several times before. He knew the place well and only came at night. He made sure to hide his face in a hoodie and kept a baseball cap pulled low over his head.

He stood in an alley between two rows of buildings, watching the white-painted signboard of the nail parlour, raindrops coursing down its side. In the flat above, the blue light was on by the small window, and the curtains were open. That was the signal that they were open for business tonight.

Under England's laws, sex work as a profession wasn't illegal. But soliciting for it was. Sex workers could be arrested if they hung around on street corners. So now they had moved indoors and online.

If anything, it had made the Watcher's job easier. Fewer witnesses to see him pick up women.

Now, he stood outside the door, his hands buried deep in his jacket pockets, his breath curling in the cold night air. He knocked three times rapidly, then three times slowly but louder, and then twice, softly again. It was the code the man inside listened for.

This was where he had first seen Anika. He had worked his magic on her. Taken her away from that hopeless idiot, Martin Keane. Ultimately, he had set Anika free, like the others.

Now it was time for another lucky woman to meet him.

He couldn't wait.

The door opened. The man from the restaurant stood there, squinting. There was a dim light behind the man, and none on the porch. The man recognised him and stood to one side. The Watcher relaxed. For a brief, paranoid moment, he wondered if the man knew about Anika. But he wouldn't let him in if he did. Ergo, either he didn't know, or he didn't care.

The Watcher stepped into the narrow landing. The man patted him down, looking for weapons. It was a thorough search. Then the man straightened and went upstairs slowly. The Watcher followed.

In the lounge upstairs, three women and two men sat on cheap sofas. One of the men was kissing a woman, and the other two were sitting still. Their faces were heavily made up, but their expressions were frozen and tired, bored almost.

He chose the woman closest to him, who smiled at him uncertainly as he approached. She was South Asian, Indian perhaps, unlike the white woman sat next to her. He thought the white woman was Polish, but he ignored her. His eyes were fixed on the Indian woman.

She had glistening, jet-black hair and lovely dark eyes. Shapely eyebrows, and skin the colour of honey. She would be a perfect replacement for Anika.

"What's your name?" he asked.

The woman stood up. She was short, no more than five feet three. The Watcher wasn't a tall man himself, but he was still bigger than the woman. He didn't like tall women. When the time came, they were difficult to subdue.

"Priya," she said. She attempted a smile. "What's yours?"

Normally, these trafficked women were subdued. They barely spoke. Clearly, Priya had some character. She smiled when he told her his name. She was no more than twenty, if that. A nice age, the Watcher thought. Perfect for his purposes.

"How are you tonight?"

"Not bad. How are you?"

"All the better for seeing you." He smiled, and she put a forced smile on her face. It didn't touch her eyes.

He pointed to the narrow hallway behind the lounge, where he knew the two bedrooms were.

"Would you like to go inside?"

The woman lowered her head and nodded. She walked ahead of him. The hallway was dimly lit by a low-powered yellow bulb in a small fitting.

Priya went inside and shut the door behind them. The Watcher stood next to the bed, and the woman started to get undressed.

"No, wait," he said.

She stopped, looking at him in surprise. Then, a sudden fear jolted in her eyes as he stepped closer to her. Her hands were bunched at her waist.

He smiled, trying to put her at ease.

"Are you alright?" he asked softly, his voice gentle.

She startled, her dark eyes wide with fear. "I—I'm fine," she stammered.

"You don't look fine," he said, reaching into his pocket. He pulled out five twenty-pound notes. "Here. Take this."

Her eyes flickered to the money, then back to him. She hesitated, unsure whether to accept.

"It's okay," he said, keeping his tone low and soothing. "I'm not here to hurt you. Take it. Get yourself something to eat."

Slowly, she reached out, her fingers brushing against his as she took the money. Her hand lingered for a moment longer than necessary.

"Priya," he repeated, testing the name on his tongue. "That's a beautiful name."

"You don't have to stay here, you know," he said, taking a small step closer. "There are better places. Better people."

Priya's brow furrowed. "I—I don't have anywhere else to go."

"Everyone has somewhere," he said. "You just need someone to help you find it."

Her eyes filled with tears, and she looked away quickly, blinking them back. "I can't leave. They won't let me."

"They can't stop you," he said firmly. "Not if you're careful."

Her gaze snapped back to his, hope flickering in her expression. "Why would you help me?"

He smiled faintly, tilting his head. "Because no one else will."

He could see that she didn't believe him. She clutched the money tightly in her hand, her shoulders relaxing slightly. Then the sound of footsteps echoed from the hall, and her posture stiffened again, the fear returning.

"Shall we…"

He shook his head. Footsteps had stopped outside the door. The Watcher jumped on the bed and started making loud grunting noises. After a while, the man outside walked away.

He thought he could see a glimmer of amusement in Priya's eyes.

"See?" he whispered, getting closer. "That's how you do it."

He ran a hand down her face, and she flinched at first but then warmed to his touch.

"That's a good girl," he whispered. "I want to be your friend, okay? Will you be my friend?"

Priya stared at him, as if she was trying to understand what this strange man was up to. Then she nodded once.

"I want to set you free," he whispered.

Priya's smooth forehead contracted. "What do you mean?"

"You want to get out of here, don't you? To be free?"

A light dawned on Priya's face, and it became brighter. Then her eyes narrowed. "Are you the police?"

"No," the Watcher smiled. "I just like to help people."

"How?"

"I'll show you. Just trust me. Keep saving up the money I'm giving you. I'll send you a phone, and you have to hide it carefully. Okay?"

Priya took a deep breath, a trace of hope lifting her sad features. "Really?"

"Yes, really. I'll come tomorrow again. Be ready for me."

"Okay."

The Watcher pulled her closer and ran his hands down her face, then across her chest and into her abdomen. It wasn't sexual; he was trying to memorise her body with his touch. She trembled and gasped, but he held her steady.

He whispered to her.

"Just relax. There you go."

He stood finally, his face inches from hers. She looked scared. He cupped her cheeks, then kissed her forehead affectionately.

"See? That wasn't bad, was it?"

She was frozen, her breathing rapid. But she shook her head to agree with him. "No."

She checked her watch.

"I have to go," she whispered, stepping away. "Thank you."

She watched him for a while. He knew she didn't trust him yet.

But that was okay.

They never did, at first.

Soon, she would.

And then, she would be his.

CHAPTER 32

Richard and Rizwan were on their way to the Taj Mahal restaurant. Rizwan drove while Richard spoke on the phone to the uniforms team who were patrolling the Barrowcliff area, near Anika's previous house.

"Nowt as yet," Richard said, hanging up the phone. "That lad Rafik's done a runner, I reckon. No one's seen him, and he's not on CCTV."

"What about Gary Faulkes?"

"The car might be off-road. They know we're looking for them. Word spreads, right?"

"But how?" Rizwan mused as he came to a stop at a red traffic light. "I mean, I know we went to the restaurant and asked the neighbours. Do you think that alerted them?"

"And the pub. Those skinheads, and the other punters. You said the guv spoke to an old man, and the pub manager?"

"Yes." The lights changed, and Rizwan tickled the accelerator. "But they'd be too scared to talk. I guess Rafik heard from the restaurant. Maybe the manager, Sachin, alerted him."

"But he told us as well. Sachin's running scared, too. Oh well. Let's get hold of both him and Priya."

At the restaurant, the lights were off, which wasn't surprising given it was only two in the afternoon. The door was locked, and when Richard leaned on the doorbell, they heard the faint buzz inside, but no one appeared.

"I'll go around the back," Rizwan said. He set off to the end of the block and then jogged around the corner, where there was an alley that ran behind the houses and shops. At this end, it was mostly shops and businesses. Rizwan found the back entrance. It looked shut.

He walked past the large, blue trash cans. There were four of them, with blue, orange and black-coloured lids. They were large enough for a man to hide in, easily. Or to store a dead body.

On an impulse, he walked over to them. They were above his chest height. He lifted the lids one by one, pinching his nose and bracing himself. He found the usual collection of bin bags and other rubbish. No dead bodies, or hiding suspects.

He tried the rear entrance, which was locked. This was used by the staff – it was white, paint flaking, chipped in all the corners. But the lock held firm. Rizwan banged on it.

His radio buzzed, and it was Richard.

"Any luck?"

"Nope."

"I'm standing on the other side of the road and looking at the upstairs window," Richard said. "The curtains are drawn, but there was a light on that just got switched off."

Rizwan's eyes fell on the narrow, black, iron-grilled staircase that went upstairs. It was round the side, behind the trash cans, and he had missed it. A grill iron landing upstairs led to another miserable white door. The windows were shut.

"There's a staircase here. I'm going upstairs."

"I'm coming over."

Rizwan went between two stinking rubbish dumpsters and went up the stairs. It was wet with rain, and he held on to the rickety railing. At the top, the door was locked when he turned the handle.

He heard a sound and looked down. Richard climbed up and joined him on the narrow landing. He peered in through the window. No curtains here, and he could see a small kitchen. It was empty, but he thought a shadow passed inside, in the corridor.

He nodded at Rizwan, who knocked loudly on the door. Richard was on the radio, calling for backup.

Rizwan thumped on the door. "This is the police! Open up!"

They heard the thud of footsteps inside, then a muted crash.

Richard swore and clambered down the stairs.

"Break it down," he ordered Rizwan as he ran for the front entrance.

Rizwan gave the door two good kicks, then leaned in with his shoulder. The lock gave way, and the door jamb splintered. The kitchen was empty. He ran into the small hallway. Two rooms branched out to his left, and a smaller door, which he thought was the loo.

Opposite the bathroom, there was a staircase, and he heard a door slam. He hoped Richard could get whoever was trying to escape.

He went into the first room. It was a bedroom with two single beds. The curtains were drawn, and the room was dark. On one of the beds, a woman sat with her knees drawn to her chin, looking scared out of her wits.

She had long black hair that was open, and she was young, in her twenties. Rizwan thought she was very beautiful, with her big dark eyes and oval face. She shrank away as he stepped closer.

He stopped and spun around when he heard a sound. It was a door opening somewhere, followed by shouts and curses. They came from downstairs. He also heard a car screeching to a stop outside.

He went to the window and pulled the flimsy curtains to one side. A squad car had blocked the road, and its doors were open. Two uniformed officers were helping Richard hold a man down on the road. They handcuffed him and hauled him to his feet.

Rizwan turned back to the woman, who was watching him with wide eyes.

"My name is DC Ahmed, of North Yorkshire Police," Rizwan said. "Don't worry. You're going to be safe now. What's your name?"

"Sheila."

"Right. Do you know a woman called Priya? She worked as a waitress downstairs."

Sheila nodded, fear still etched in her face. "She's not here. I don't know where she is."

CHAPTER 33

Rita stood outside in the garden as the wail of sirens grew louder. DI Ahmed stood next to her. They had searched around the mansion, which had eight bedrooms, a garage with a Ferrari and two Range Rovers, and an outhouse opposite the conservatory. The entire house was empty. It looked like only Yosef lived here. But Rita also found evidence of bondage gear in a bedroom, which had been converted into a makeshift studio. The bedsheets were crumpled, and the ensuite bathroom had a shaving kit inside it. The bath had been used recently.

Rita called Harper, who answered. He was shocked at the news.

"I'm at the Modern Slavery Unit HQ in Leeds. I've got a couple of meetings, but I'm coming over."

"You don't have to," Rita said.

"No, this is important. Whoever killed Yosef knew he had to be silenced urgently. I'll see you in less than an hour."

Rita hung up and joined DI Ahmed as he went back inside the property with the uniformed officers, who were setting up a crime scene perimeter.

They had shoe coverings on and wore gloves. Rita was careful not to touch anything. Her eyes fell on the camera that faced the rear garden. She walked around and found cameras facing the front and sides as well. In the large, marble-floored reception area, she found more cameras. Under the staircase, in a cupboard, she located the electric circuit. The large red switch at the end was turned down. She flicked it up, then came out and tried the lights. They didn't work. It was late afternoon, three p.m., but there was still light in the sky.

She went outside and called DI Ahmed. "Someone's tampered with the electric wires. Can we check the main wires that supply the house? They'll be on the street."

Ahmed had a look under the cupboard, at the circuit box. "The main electric cable comes out underground. It will be somewhere under the circuit board. Have we checked in the basement?"

Rita hadn't, so she went downstairs with Ahmed and two uniformed officers. The basement was cavernous, and part of it was half dug for a swimming pool. Rita followed Ahmed, who led the way with a flashlight. He stopped when the uniformed officer pointed his light at a white boxed cabling that went up the wall towards the ground floor. It had been hacked, as if with a saw. Ahmed reached out a hand and pulled at one of the severed black, green, and blue wires. He was careful not to touch the open end.

"Someone cut off the electricity to this place," he said, his voice echoing in the dark, gloomy hall. Rita watched their shadows loom in the blackness around them, her mind racing.

"The killer planned this. He wanted to destroy any CCTV evidence before he came in to kill Yosef."

"Or after," Ahmed said. "If the CCTV is hard-wired, and he's hacked the wires, chances are the footage is also gone."

They went upstairs and checked the cameras and searched for the CCTV monitors. Eventually, one of the uniforms found the monitors in another section of the basement.

"Looks like the cameras were wire-connected to the mains, guv," the uniformed sergeant said. "I doubt we'll get anything from the cameras."

Rita nodded and went outside to call the lads and gave them the news.

"Yes, Yosef is dead," she told an unbelieving Richard. "Battered with what looks like a cricket or baseball bat. It was vicious, his face is smashed to pulp. I could just about recognise him from the photos. DI Ahmed confirms it's him."

"Okay," Richard said slowly. "Wait till you hear what we found at the restaurant." He told Rita about their trip to the Taj Mahal.

"We got Sachin. He was hiding in the restaurant and tried to escape. He's in custody, and we also found a woman called Sheila Shetty. I've called the Modern Slavery Unit, and they said they would inform Harper."

"He's on his way here. See what you can get out of Sachin. I'm glad you caught him before he suffered the same fate as Yosef. This other woman you found there—Sheila—has she shed any light on the trafficking gang so far?"

"We haven't really spoken to her as yet. Rizwan and I will try, but it might be easier when you're here. I think she's scared of us. But she has given us her family's details in India."

"Get in touch with them now." Rita checked her watch. It was getting close to five p.m. "It will be around half ten p.m. there now. But no time like the present. As long as you're sure they are her family—tell them and arrange for them to come over when they can. I guess you have to liaise with Modern Slavery for that."

When she hung up, Harper had arrived. He was speaking to DI Ahmed, and they watched two Scene of Crime officers, in their sterile white suits, step inside the ring of the central crime scene, where Yosef's battered body still lay in the same position. Harper saw Rita and hurried over.

"I came as soon as I could. Did you find him like this?"

"Yes. And that's not all. We got Sachin, at the Taj Mahal in Scarborough." Rita told him what Riz and Richard had found.

"Any sign of Rafik?" Harper asked.

"Not yet. But he can't be far, even if he's tried to escape."

"Fantastic," Harper beamed, his eyes glistening. "Looks like you're dismantling the network now. Don't need me anymore, do you?" He chuckled.

"Well, we do need you to find out who did this," Rita pointed at the conservatory, where Yosef's body lay.

The smile faded from Harper's lips. "Yes. This is strange. I always thought Yosef was one of the masterminds of the network. And he still might be, but clearly, there's someone above him."

"Exactly. And that person can come and go as he or she pleases. I doubt we'll get any CCTV footage of what happened, despite all the cameras here."

"Yes, Ahmed just told me about the cut cables. I think this wasn't the work of one person, it was a team. To get in, cut the cables, kill Yosef—all of that would take some time."

"Hopefully, Scene of Crime will show something," Rita said, watching the white-suited forensic officers at work. Harper was scrolling on his phone.

"I've got messages from MSU HQ in Leeds. Your DC reported to them."

"Yes, he did. Does your HQ have any more information on Rafik? Can they trace him?"

"They're trying. He's being clever. He's not using his credit cards or any phone number previously associated with him. Where do you think he might be?"

"Like I said, nearby. If Sachin was at the restaurant, with that girl, Rafik won't be that far. I think the boss of this operation needs Rafik to move the women around. And Gary Faulkes."

"Yes. We need to find both of them."

Rita sighed. "Shall we head back to Scarborough? Sachin's in custody now, and I'm looking forward to interrogating him. I need you to arrange for the repatriation of Sheila. And we still haven't found the other woman, Priya."

Rita's phone rang again. It was Richard. "Guv, wait till you hear this."

CHAPTER 34

Rita took the train back, as Harper had to return to Leeds. Yosef's murder investigation was now under West Yorkshire Police jurisdiction, but DI Ahmed had promised her he would keep her in the loop.

By the time Rita returned to Scarborough, it was dark. Rizwan was waiting for her, and they sped over to Eastfield. Riz put the siren on and made short work of the few miles southeast from the train station to the suburb of Eastfield. It was a poverty- and crime-ridden area. Many shop windows on the High Street were boarded up, and a gang of youths stood at a street corner, dispersing when they saw the car.

Rizwan pulled up on Havers Hill, a road that ran through a council estate. This section of the long road had a row of terraced houses. They were reasonably well maintained, from what Rita could see under the streetlights. Two squad cars stood outside the terraced house, which had been converted into a ground-floor and upstairs flat, like several houses on the street.

"What have we found?" Rita asked as she hurried over to the front door with Rizwan.

"Evidence of several people living here. Sheila Shetty told us the address, and Sunil confirmed it. He doesn't know where Rafik is, by the way. But Sheila told us Rafik came here on a regular basis."

A uniformed inspector stood guard at the door. Rita recognised Steve Bennett.

"No sign of anyone inside," Steve said. "But it looks a sorry sight."

Rita nodded, put her gloves, apron, and shoe covers on, and went inside. The flat downstairs had two bedrooms, a kitchen, and a bathroom, with a living room that was small and cramped. The place was a mess, with carpet missing from the floor, and open suitcases overflowing with clothes, as if they had been emptied and searched. Plaster had fallen from the walls, and damp spread across them, mould growing in the corners. Rita put a hand over her nose as she entered the bedroom. She counted five mattresses on the floor, and some of them had been slept in.

"Sheila said six of them stayed in the ground-floor apartment, and several more upstairs. Priya and herself were upstairs, with another two. Ten women in total lived here. They used to be in the house in Barrowcliff."

"And now they've moved again," Rita said, coming out of the stuffy bedroom. She went outside and dragged a breath of fresh air into her lungs. She put her hands on her hips and looked upstairs. There was a light in the window, and she could see a familiar shape appear. It was Richard. She waved at him, and he waved back.

"When did you get here?" she asked Rizwan.

"About an hour ago. Both the flats were empty. We raided this place as soon as Sheila gave us the location."

"But they knew they had to vacate this place as well. How did they know?"

From Rizwan's silent face, she knew he didn't have the answer. An uncomfortable feeling was growing inside her, spreading tentacles of disquiet.

"Maybe that's why Sheila was moved to the flat above the restaurant," Rita carried on. "What happened to Priya?"

"Sheila doesn't know. Priya left before the men came—Sachin and Rafik. Rafik took some of the women elsewhere, and Sachin took Sheila to the restaurant. She thinks Priya is on her own, out there somewhere."

Rita tapped her foot on the ground. "So they moved out even before you went back to the Taj Mahal. Ergo, they thought even this hiding place was gone." Rita rubbed her forehead. A headache was growing, like the pangs of hunger in her belly. "Let's have a look upstairs and head back to base."

The flat upstairs was smaller, with the second bedroom basically a box room. The larger bedroom had three mattresses on the floor. There was no carpet, and the place looked like it had been hit by a bomb. Wallpaper peeled from the walls, the windows were cracked, and there was an overpowering smell of rot.

Richard joined them in the lounge. Perspiration caked his forehead, and he breathed heavily.

"No sign of any laptops or phones. We searched the whole place."

"They knew they had to clear out. At least we have them on the run. But we need to find the other women."

"Three men as well," Richard said, and Rizwan nodded. "Young boys really, just turned nineteen. Big dreams of making it to the land of opportunity," Richard grimaced and shook his head. "If they cleared out of here, I wonder what they might do to the others. Get rid of them?"

"Let's hope not," Rita said, a coldness seeping into her limbs. "I'll see you back at the base."

CHAPTER 35

Rita picked up a salad from the canteen and wolfed it down at the office. Jack had called, and she spoke to him quickly.

"I'm with a client in custody," he said. "I can see you after you finish if you like. Just to give you a lift back home because, as you know, I'm your designated chauffeur."

Rita smiled at that. "At least you know your place."

"I do need a bonus, however. There's a cost of living crisis going on, unless you've noticed. Alright for a rich Detective Inspector like you."

"Just keep my Rolls-Royce clean and ready, like a good chauffeur, okay?"

"Don't forget the bonus. If not cash, I want it in kind. Alright?"

The cheeky man was pushing boundaries, Rita thought with a shake of her head. "Call me later," she said.

"Good luck with interviewing the suspects. I bumped into Steve Bennett. You didn't find anyone at the house in Eastfield, did you? Just like you didn't in Barrowcliff."

"No," Rita said slowly.

"I think you have a mole," Richard said softly, his voice low. "Someone is warning the gang in advance. Or they're extremely well prepared. Isn't the Modern Slavery Unit helping?"

"Yes, they are. DI James Harper's joined us. He'll be back tomorrow to help." Rita told Jack about Yosef's death.

"More evidence of an inside job," Jack said. "We have an office in Leeds. One of our partners was part of the prosecution against a gang of traffickers like these. I'll speak to him tonight, see if he can help."

"Thanks, Jack. I'll see you soon."

"Keep my bonus ready," he laughed and hung up.

Rita finished her salad while Richard and Rizwan returned. They looked tired. Richard yawned and passed a hand over his face.

"Sachin's got a duty solicitor. Do you want to see him first, or Sheila?"

"Sheila. What about Martin?"

"He's still here, but we need to let him go first thing tomorrow."

"That's fine. I don't think he did it, anyway. And he was in custody when Yosef was killed. He's not who we're looking for. But let's lean on him tomorrow for one last time, see if he knows anything about Rafik or the gang."

Rita went down to the custody chambers and checked on Sheila. She was in the minimal security zone, and a female uniformed constable stood guard outside her cell. The door was open, unlike for other arrested criminals. Sheila was sitting on the bed, and her eyes were wide with fear as she watched Rita enter. Rita shut the door behind her.

Sheila was young, in her early twenties. Her long hair was unwashed and straggly, and she had no makeup, but she was still beautiful.

"You're going home," Rita said. "Don't worry. The nightmare is over for you. My team have spoken to your parents, and you will speak to them soon as well. Alright?"

Tears budded in Sheila's eyes and streamed down her face. She held her head in her hands and sobbed. Rita gave her some time.

"Where is Priya?"

"I don't know. She stood up to Rafik when he was hitting me. Then she left. She wasn't there when Rafik and Sachin returned. She didn't tell me where she was going."

"Does she have a phone?" Rita remembered Anika's phone, washed up on the beach. "Did she have any money?"

"Yes, she had a phone. That was a secret she shared with me. As for money, the men gave us twenty pounds spending money every week. We saved up some to get a phone, but the men searched us regularly—our beds, wardrobes. They found a phone that we bought for cash, but the men found it. Then they…"

Sheila bit her lip and looked down.

Rita's heart broke for her. "They hurt you?" she said softly.

Without looking up, Sheila nodded. Rita closed her eyes. Sadness and rage battered her heart, and her jaw flexed as she thought of the animals who did this. She wouldn't rest until she brought them to justice.

"Help me to find them, Sheila. Can you think of anything else? They had a boss from whom they took orders. Did you ever see him?"

"No."

"We know that Anika was seeing a man called Martin. Did you or Priya have a man like that?"

Sheila frowned then and narrowed her eyes.

"What is it?" Rita asked when she didn't speak.

"Priya knew a man. He was a customer, but Priya had grown close to him. I don't know who he is. But he helped to get her a phone and keep it for her. She met him a couple of times. I asked her again recently, but she didn't say anything."

"When did she tell you this?"

"Recently. About three days ago."

The day of Anika's murder, Rita thought to herself. A chill entered her spine and worked its way up to her brain. Could Anika's killer now be fixated on Priya?

"Sheila, this is important. Can you think of anything Priya might have told you about this man? Was he young or old? White or Asian?"

Sheila bit her bottom lip again and thought hard. "He was white. She told me that much. Nothing about his age or where he lived."

"Where did she see him?"

"Well, there's this flat in town, above a shop near the Taj Mahal restaurant. That's where we…" Sheila's words drifted off into silence.

Rita was now getting her hopes up. If it was in the town centre, she could get CCTV evidence—maybe.

"You said three days ago. Today is Thursday, 5th October. Do you mean Tuesday, 3rd October? Think carefully. Did you see Anika that day, for instance?"

Sheila shook her head. "No, we didn't see Anika. I'm sorry, it wasn't Tuesday. It was Wednesday. Sorry, I got confused."

"No problem," Rita said, her heart beating faster now. "So, yesterday, Wednesday, you think Priya met this man, right? At the flat above the shop? What's the name of the shop?" The questions were tumbling out of Rita. She needed to find Priya before the worst happened.

"It's a nail bar called *All That Glitters*. It was late, after the dinner shift at the restaurant. She was working there, and when we do an evening shift there, we are taken to the flat above the nail bar or to a house in Barrowcliff. But Priya told me this morning she met the man above the nail bar flat."

"Do you think Priya might be with that man now?"

"I don't know." Sheila looked helpless. "Maybe."

Rita went up to the ground floor and ran down the corridor. A storm of anxiety was brewing in her mind, dark clouds and thunder flashing. In the illumination, she could see the landscape, and it was macabre, cold. She was beginning to understand why the cold case with the same MO as Anika's was an unidentified woman.

The man who killed them thrived on finding lost, forsaken women on the fringes of society—women no one would miss, who had no family. He had probably killed several more, if not hundreds. Only two had been reported so far. With Anika, he had gone too far, probably seeking recognition of his work. That's how these malignant narcissistic personalities worked.

Rita flung open the office door, only to find it empty. There was a note on Richard's desk—*Gone to interview Sachin.*

Rita cursed; she had missed them downstairs in the custody chambers. She felt exhausted, sweat pooling at the back of her neck. She wanted nothing more than to lie down and close her eyes. The headache was gathering force, sharpening to a pinpoint in the middle of her eyes. She snapped her eyes shut and massaged her forehead, which didn't help.

Two cases had been reported so far… and she had no intention of letting Priya become the third.

She went outside, walked rapidly down the corridor, and then ran up the stairs to the third floor, where Traffic had their HQ. She held her fob key against the glass double doors, and they swung open.

The row of desks and chairs was mostly empty, save for two occupied by the duty team at the front. They faced a bank of CCTV monitors covering the entire wall.

Rita walked over to the duty sergeant, whose name badge said *Connelly*. She smiled at Rita. "Working late, guv?"

"I've got an urgent situation," Rita said, pulling up a chair. "I need some footage of a suspect from a high street location. The date is Wednesday—yesterday—and the time will be after midnight. It's a nail bar called *All That Glitters*, and I've got the address here."

"OK, hold on."

Rita waited while Connelly did the search on her system. Soon, the colour boxes on her monitor changed, and the views of a dark street appeared. The time stamp was midnight. On the right side of the street, Rita saw a row of shops, and the white sign of the nail bar was visible.

"Speed up a little," Rita said. "I want to see the views after half past midnight."

Connelly did as told. At four minutes past one in the morning, there was a hit. A figure crossed the street. He stopped and looked around, his back hunched against the cold. He wore a grey anorak, and the hood was pulled over his head. Any sort of identification was impossible. But Rita watched his gait. There was something familiar about it. He walked slowly, the gait of an older man. A door next to the nail bar opened, and he went inside. That door clearly belonged to the same property and probably led upstairs or had a side entrance to the ground floor.

"Keep tracking," Rita said. "I want to see when he comes out. Is there a back exit or entrance?"

"I'll have a look on the other cameras."

After ten minutes of looking at different angles, and Rita checking the map on her camera, they made certain the property didn't have a back entrance that emerged onto a street. It backed onto an alley that lay between terraced houses.

Connelly switched back to the front view of the nail bar. Finally, she stopped her scrolling. The man appeared again, the hood lowered low over his head. He shoved his hands in his pockets and started walking. Again, Rita found that gait familiar.

Then she looked at his feet.

And the revelation hit her like a sledgehammer in the guts.

CHAPTER 36

Rita asked Connelly to send her the images, then she raced down the stairs. She bumped into Jack at the bottom of the staircase—literally smacked right into him. She was immediately embarrassed.

"I'm so sorry."

"Whoa, no problem," Jack said, holding his arms up. He scanned her face, and then his eyebrows lowered.

"What's going on? You look majorly stressed."

He matched Rita's pace as she half-walked, half-ran to the office.

"I think I've found the killer."

She burst into the office, and Rizwan and Richard were at their desks. They were startled by Rita's entrance, followed by Jack. They listened to Rita, concern growing on their faces. Then they looked at each other.

Rita said, "I've asked Traffic to put out an APB (All Points Bulletin) for him. But I'm worried he might escape in a new car and use a burner phone."

There was a knowing look in Richard's eye as he glanced at Rizwan again. Rita didn't miss it.

"What's going on?"

Richard said, "We spoke to Sachin. He insists he's just a junior member of the gang, and he only takes the women around and manages the restaurant. His boss was Yosef. But he told us about a man in a blue van who came to see Anika. He came twice, Sachin said, and he parked the blue van in a side alley without any CCTV cameras. Hence, we don't have the registration number, but there's a chance it's the same blue van that was seen on the night of Anika's murder."

"And what about the man?"

"He's old, maybe in his sixties. Caucasian, about five feet nine, and the peculiar thing about him was that he—"

"Wore slippers on his feet," Rita finished, her eyes shining, veins brimming with adrenaline. "Is that correct?"

"Yes."

"Paul Manning," Rita said softly. "I can't believe it. But it makes sense. He would've known Anika as a sex worker, and if she came to Roshni to seek help, he probably saw her there as well."

Rita looked at Rizwan. "Get me the reg number of the blue van, and let's see if we can find it on CCTV. What are the chances that he's going to use the same van again?"

Jack spoke from the door. "I'm not part of this case, but if we're speaking of this killer, he's going to be a creature of habit. He likes his routine."

Rita agreed. "And there's a strong chance he's taken Priya in that van tonight. You two go upstairs while I call Poonam."

Rita had Poonam's number, and to her relief, the woman answered. Her voice was cautious. "Who's this?"

"DI Rita Gupta. I have something urgent to discuss with you."

Briefly, she explained what she had seen on CCTV.

"Does Paul drive a blue van?"

She sensed Poonam's shock; the woman could barely speak. "Yes," she finally whispered. "But not always. I've seen him drive it only at night. He picked up supplies from the store once and brought them to our offices. I stayed back late to keep the door open for him."

"Think carefully, Poonam. Have you ever seen Paul with any of the women who came to the centre? Or anything strange that you might have noticed that you haven't told us yet? Please don't hold back."

Poonam was quiet for a while, and Rita heard her breathing heavily. "I haven't seen him with another woman, but his ex-wife once said something that I remembered."

"Ex-wife? I thought he was still married?"

"That's the impression he gave you at the office, I know. But he's been divorced for many years. I knew Diane, his ex-wife. She... she told me once he could get aggressive. He held her by the throat once and told her if she didn't have sex with him, he might go out and kill someone. He apologised later, and he was drunk."

"What?" Rita was incredulous. "And she didn't tell this to the police? Or the lawyers?"

"She said it was only once. They divorced shortly after. This was back in Bradford, many years ago." Poonam stopped suddenly, then spoke after a beat. "She also said that in those days, Paul stayed out late quite often. He drove a minicab at night after his day job in the paper mill factory."

Rita made a mental note to check for cold cases in Bradford. But she had more pressing matters at hand.

"Do you know where Paul lives?"

"In Scalby. He has a house there. I've never been, but he's sent supplies from there, and I've seen his card. Would you like the address?"

"Yes, please. And do you know where he is right now? Do you know anyone who might know, if you don't?"

Poonam spoke slowly. "No. But Paul was at the office this afternoon. He seemed very happy with himself. I thought he got some funding from the council for a new office. But he said he didn't. He left and said he was going into town."

"What time was this?"

"Around four pm."

"And was he driving the blue van?"

"No. He had his usual car, a grey Honda. I saw him drive out of the parking spot in front of the office. That's the last I saw of him."

Rita thought quickly. "I need the CCTV camera footage from your office, for the registration number of the car. This is important, Poonam. I wouldn't be asking if it wasn't."

"It's alright, I don't mind. Are you sure about this? Do you really think it was Paul who did that to Anika?"

"We have eyewitness evidence of Paul going to see Anika, and he was at the same brothel last night. We know he was with Priya, the woman who's missing now. I know it's Paul. We have to find him quickly—I'm very concerned he has Priya."

"I'm going now. Shall I send you the footage as soon as I have it?"

"Yes, please."

The phone on Rita's desk was ringing, and Jack snatched it up. "We got the blue van on CCTV," Rizwan said breathlessly.

CHAPTER 37

Connelly jabbed a finger at the screen in front of her. "There it is."

The blue van was hidden in the alley four streets down from the nail bar, *All That Glitters.* Connelly zoomed in and magnified the image to read the registration number on the plate.

"It's been to this location regularly over the last six months," she explained. A constable had joined her, and they had run a search on ANPR for the blue van. Two large screens, each divided into twelve boxes, showed the blue van, under cover of darkness, parked in the same spot at night.

"Okay," Rita said impatiently. "But what about now? Where have you spotted him?"

"On the A170, Pickering to Thirsk Road," Richard said.

Connelly pushed her chair back to her own desk and brought up the live images. The A170 was an important road link, a line on the map that ran from the sea and Scarborough on the left to Thirsk, a major town, on the right.

Rita only saw a dark stretch of the dual carriageway, but then she saw the van. It had stopped on the side of the road, in a lay-by well covered by trees.

Connelly changed the views, and they saw the van from the opposite angle. It was mostly obscured by the undergrowth, but still visible. A grey Honda was parked in front of it. As she watched, a man got out from the driver's seat of the Honda, and a woman from the passenger side.

"That's Priya and Paul," Rita whispered. Her heart pounded as she watched the couple get into the blue van and drive off.

"This happened at 19:26 hours," Connelly said. "Half an hour ago." She tracked the blue van, and they watched as it took a right turn onto a road whose sign Rita couldn't read.

"That's the Rosedale Chimney Bank Road," Connelly said. "It's a long, narrow path that goes up to the old Rosedale mines."

"Where we found the cold case," Rizwan whispered. "Near the old iron ore mines in Rosedale."

They all looked at each other, and Rita felt a surge of adrenaline spike in her blood.

"It's not great at this time of night. It climbs sharply, and there are no streetlights."

Sparks of fear crashed against Rita's spine, her pulse racing as she stared at the blue van disappearing onto Chimney Bank Road, swallowed by the darkness.

"We need to get moving. He's choosing the same location as he did with the cold case three years ago. We need to stop him."

Rita rang switchboard and asked to be connected to the duty uniforms team. Inspector Mark Botley was on call, and Rita had worked with him in the past.

"I'll send a unit out," Botley said. "The terrain's rough out there. No lights on the road. If you really want to catch this guy, we're going to need some aerial support."

"I'll speak to my boss about contacting NPAS. We should be able to get a bird up there. I need a lift to the location. Can one of your units help?"

"They're both on patrol, and they'd have to come back to base, which would lose time."

Rita looked at Richard and Riz. "Do either of you have a car?"

Rizwan had a gleam in his eye. "I do. My A3 is the sports version, so it's got a sixteen-valve engine and—"

"Save it, Riz," Rita raised a hand. "If the answer is yes, then let's get going."

The National Police Air Service was the centralised, 24/7 helicopter service for all of England's police forces. Rita rang Nicola Perkins, who wasn't happy to be disturbed. She listened to Rita in silence.

"And what evidence do you have that Paul Manning has actually abducted this woman and that she's at risk of losing her life?"

"We have him on CCTV, and given his MO with Anika and the cold case, the chances of Priya meeting the same end are very high."

Nicola was quiet for a while. Rita screwed her fingers into a fist in frustration. She didn't have time on her side.

"And you're sure Paul Manning was the man who was seen with the victim?"

"Positive. And he was with her yesterday as well."

"Okay," Nicola said, and Rita could've punched the air in joy. She couldn't contact NPAS without her boss's approval. She rang NPAS's central switchboard, gave her name, rank, and location. Then she waited. Connelly was still scanning different screens, but most of Rosedale Chimney Bank Road lay in CCTV dark spots.

Rita synced her radio to the correct channel with Connelly. She and her constable would provide them with real-time information as they drove to Rosedale.

Jack was still downstairs, and Rita felt a bit bad for leaving him behind. But Jack wasn't a police officer, and she couldn't get him clearance for assisting in an op that could put him in danger.

"I can follow you guys," Jack said, giving her a wink.

"No," Rita said firmly.

She was on her way out, and Jack walked to the car park with her. She knew he was joking with his offer in any case. He stopped and grabbed both her shoulders as Rizwan got the car around.

"Good luck," Jack whispered. "And don't do anything stupid."

"Like jump into a mineshaft?" Rita grinned as she got into the back seat. "We'll be fine, don't worry."

She watched as Jack stood in the car park, his figure becoming smaller. It was nice to know he cared.

She put her mind to more urgent matters. Her radio was flashing its red light on top, and she pulled it out, turning the black knob to the right.

"NPAS to DI Gupta."

"DI Gupta receiving."

"We are on standby to dispatch on your order. We will be taking off from Carr Gate base, north of Doncaster. ETA to Rosedale Chimney Bank is thirty minutes."

"No, wait. I want the helicopter to search for a blue van on Chimney Bank Road, off the A170 Pickering to Thirsk Road."

Richard helped Rita with the precise location, sending it to the NPAS base as a link.

"Roger that," the switchboard operator said. "Your next call will be from the helicopter pilot and support crew."

Rita hung up.

Rizwan had tickled the accelerator, and the car hurtled through the night, overtaking other vehicles so fast it left them almost at a standstill. The engine whined, and the lights on the A170 became a blur.

Rizwan was forced to slow down as they passed the villages of Middleton and then Aislaby. Soon, the turning for Rosedale Chimney Bank arrived, the sign picked up by the headlights. There were no lights here, but Rita was surprised at the width of the road. Road markings were absent, and they plunged into the darkness, the twin beams of the headlights illuminating a broad black strip that disappeared into the void.

Rita put the window down. The air was crisp and cold, and she could smell the heather and gorse on the hills. The wind moaned between the craggy peaks, and the first drops of rain arrived. She couldn't see the hills, but their presence was palpable.

The road rose and fell, and they passed a couple of cars coming in the opposite direction. Soon thereafter, it was just them—the impenetrable night pressing through the window, and the granite shoulders of the giant hills.

Rizwan was driving slower now, but he had to slow down even further when the road narrowed. Richard and Rita took their torches out and shone them outside whenever they saw a shape by the side of the road. They passed the white sign for Rosedale Abbey. The road began to climb.

Richard raised a hand. "Stop."

Rizwan screeched to a halt. Richard shone his torch beam outside.

There, under a crop of bushes by the side of the road, was a blue van.

CHAPTER 38

"It's the same registration number," Richard said. They were standing behind the blue van, and the men had cleared the branches and undergrowth out of the way. The drizzle was steady now, falling from an invisible, inky black sky. Rita shivered in a sudden gust of wind.

Richard's torch beam was focused on the van. It moved inside the van – it was empty. There was nothing on the seats. On the driver's side, a pair of gloves lay on the dashboard under the windscreen.

There was a trampling sound of footsteps, and Rita raised her torch swiftly. She pointed it in the direction of the sound, to her left and above. The hills sloped down towards her, and she picked out a high-visibility jacket. Then another appeared, and two uniformed constables trudged slowly down the hills towards them. The ground was soft, and the mud was already clinging to the bottom of their trousers.

"PC Hopkins, ma'am," the younger constable said, touching the peak of his cap. "We arrived ten minutes before you. Seen nowt as yet, apart from the van. There's four of us, and we're searching up there, where the disused mines are. Another unit's on their way."

"Okay," Rita said. "We'll follow you up there. But I want one of you down here to watch the van. This is his getaway. Let's make sure he doesn't slip through our fingers."

As far as Rita knew, Paul wasn't aware that he was being chased. She wanted to maintain the element of surprise for as long as she could.

Pointing the beam of their lights at their feet, they trudged up the slope. The going was slow, the soft earth sucking at their rubber-soled shoes. The smell of the wet soil mingled with the heather and sagebrush, a fresh and invigorating scent. Not that Rita was in the mood for it. Her breath made fumes of attrition in the air, a wheeze rasped in her lungs. Her legs were tired, the burn in her thighs leading to an ache in her bones.

But she kept putting one foot above the other. After what seemed like an eternity, the land opened up, and a fresh breeze struck her in the face.

"We're reaching the Bank Top Kilns," PC Hopkins called out. "These are the kilns of the old factory. The mines are above, and the ground there is filled with potholes. Be careful not to fall in them – some are deep."

Great, Rita groaned. She wondered if Paul knew this terrain and had brought victims here before. It would make sense, given his MO of finding remote locations to fulfil his sick fantasies.

After another spate of climbing, they stopped at the top of the plateau. The wind was stronger here, moaning around them with greater force. The drizzle remained steady, and there was no respite from the raindrops that plastered Rita's wet hair to her forehead. She hurried closer, with an effort, to reach Hopkins. She kept her voice low, knowing sound carried in the silence.

"What about the mining shafts?"

"They're signposted, but not all of them. The villagers find dead sheep in old, unmarked shafts sometimes. We have to be careful."

A sudden, ear-splitting scream shattered the silence like a chainsaw. It came from directly ahead.

"That didn't sound very far," Rita whispered.

"The wind can be deceiving – it carries sound over longer distances," Hopkins said. "We need to hurry."

Rita knew the men were tired as well, but they renewed the force in their exhausted legs.

Hopkins and Richard moved ahead, their torch beams crisscrossing the ground. There was a new urgency in their movements now. The drizzle was lighter, but the ground remained soft. Rita tried to test the ground before putting her weight on it, but that slowed her down. Rizwan gave her a hand, and she clutched his elbow as they trudged on through the mud and darkness, in the direction of the scream.

Rita listened hard as the wind whined and whistled in her ears. Several times, she thought she heard a human voice, but they were footsteps and other night sounds carried in the wind. Then she saw a shape loom in the mid-distance to her right. Her eyes were now well adjusted to the dark, and she thought she saw a human figure appear above the shape, then vanish.

"Did you see that?" she whispered to Rizwan. He had stopped, like her. Richard and Hopkins were still moving ahead.

"Yes, I did."

Rita called for Richard, but he didn't hear. She pulled her radio out, and Hopkins answered. He stopped, and then his voice came back on the channel.

"Roger that, guv. There's someone over there. It's a rock formation over an abandoned mine quarry. I think so, anyway."

"Let's take a look. The scream came from that direction, right?"

"Correct."

"Let's go."

CHAPTER 39

Rita was exhausted by the time she got to the rock formation. They seemed to grow in size as she got closer, rising up like a granite forest, blocking out the night sky. She contacted the others on her radio.

"Spread out. Turn off the torch lights. Keep in contact."

The other three murmured their assent. Rita stepped forward slowly, ignoring the burn in her thighs every time she moved. She put a hand on the cold surface of the rock. It was smooth and wet with rain. She moved around a wide boulder and saw a raised, flat surface in front of her. It took her a little time to realise it was man-made. It was derelict, wind and rain had chipped at it for centuries. She didn't know what purpose it had served, but she felt certain it was part of the iron ore mines found here. Beyond the raised surface, the night opened up, the wind fresh and strong, and she could tell the land fell away into emptiness – was it a cliff edge? Or the start of a valley?

She clutched the extendable baton in her hand and moved again. A sound made her stop. This time, she heard the whimper clearly. A woman's voice, trying to speak, but the sound was muffled, as if she was gagged. Then she saw the human shape again, a man moving on the raised surface. She was closer now and crouched down. She moved on her hands and feet and touched the surface. It was made of old bricks. Vegetation grew between the cracks.

She crouched lower as the man's shape appeared again. He shuffled along the surface, seeming to know his way around. Rita raised her head when she heard the whimper again. About ten feet away, a shape lay on the ground. It moved, and Rita saw a woman was tied up – hands and feet – with a gag over her mouth. The man moved close by, picking up some objects from the ground. He made a small tower of what looked like decayed bricks and laid them on the ground, as if making a pattern.

Rita shuddered when she realised she was watching a serial killer at work. Paul was making a mausoleum of bricks, where he would place the woman. She must be Priya, Rita thought, but she couldn't make out her face.

Rita gripped the baton in her hand and rose silently. She put a foot on the surface, and the ground was soft. It was mostly grass, with square formations of bricks on the ground. She climbed up onto the surface and stayed low, bent at the waist. Her radio was turned down to silent. The whispering rain had started again, but it wasn't the steady drizzle as before. The wind still moaned down the craggy peaks, but it was now blocked by the rock formation, which created a shelter.

The man worked on, arranging the bricks in what seemed like a circle.

Rita crept forward, checking each step to make sure she didn't make a sound. The woman was now still, but Rita could hear her breathing heavily. She would have to wait a little longer. She lay close to the man, within his reach.

Rita could now recognise Paul's shape. She needed to make sure Paul was knocked out before she could help Priya. She hoped and prayed the others were nearby and ready to help. But if not, she would have to do this alone.

Rita was getting closer. The woman wiggled and moved, and Paul stopped suddenly. Rita froze, dropping down to her haunches. Paul stood still now, head cocked to one side, as if listening for something. He dropped the bricks from his hand, moved swiftly, and crouched by the woman, facing Rita.

"I can see you," Paul said, his voice no more than a whisper. "Come on, stand up. No point in hiding any more."

Rita rose and took a step forward. She spoke loudly. "Paul Manning. That's you, correct?"

Paul said nothing. Rita could tell he had his elbow around Priya's neck now, holding her close to his chest. As if she were something precious to him.

Rita got closer. Paul said, "I'd stop there if I were you."

"Hand her over, Paul. She's done nothing to you."

"You're that inspector, aren't you? The one who came to…" He stopped, perhaps realising that if he mentioned his office, he'd give the game away.

"That's right. I came to the Roshni office, and I saw you. How long have you been doing this, Paul? We know about the woman you buried around here. Are you planning the same for Priya?"

He said nothing. Instead, he stood, dragging Priya back with him. Rita rushed forward, her baton raised, then stopped abruptly. She'd been right about the cliff edge. Only, it wasn't a cliff, but a more shallow valley. She couldn't see a great deal, but the dense crop of treetops was evident, and while the slope was gentle, the fall would still kill or injure anyone unlucky enough to tip over the edge.

"Let her go, Paul," Rita shouted. She wiped the raindrops from her face and held the baton lower. "She's done nothing to you."

"She needs to be free," Paul said. His voice was softer, but Rita heard him. His words chilled her more than the wind and rain. "I give them freedom, Inspector. You keep them enslaved."

Rita was getting closer, and she needed to keep Paul talking. "What are you talking about? It doesn't make sense."

But he was alert to her movements. He stepped closer to the edge, pulling a whimpering, struggling Priya with him.

"If I can't set her free, I can let her go over the edge," Paul said. "Is that what you want?"

"No. She's innocent. She's suffered enough. Please let her go."

From the corner of her eye, Rita thought she detected movement. But she didn't dare move her head, aware Paul's eyes were fixed on her like a hawk.

"That's what I was doing. Letting her go. Giving her freedom. But you stopped me."

Rita heard a distant rumble in the sky, and the sound grew louder. The chopping blades of the helicopter appeared over the horizon, a light gleaming from the machine.

"It's over, Paul," Rita shouted. "Hand yourself in. There's no escape for you."

Paul made a high-pitched sound, and Rita realised he was laughing. "You think I want to escape? No, I want recognition. I helped these women to get freedom from their horrible lives. They can escape – not me."

Paul moved even closer to the edge, and Rita gasped when she saw the loose pieces of rock crumble and fall. She saw the flicker of movement behind Paul again, and this time, she looked. Paul followed her movement, and he was distracted momentarily as he glanced behind him.

Rita ran forward and lunged for Paul.

CHAPTER 40

Paul realised he was being attacked from both directions. He grunted and tried to shove Priya over the edge. But Rita landed on Priya's legs and gripped them tightly.

Two shadows rose up behind Paul. One grabbed his knees, bringing him to the ground, while the other pushed him forward by the shoulders.

Paul screamed and shouted, then fought back. He didn't let go of Priya, but neither could he move her, as Rita was holding her legs steady. They fell on top of each other in a tangled heap. Rita felt something blunt hit her on the head, and she moved to one side. She caught the glint of a metallic object in the air.

"He's got a knife!" she screamed.

She saw the knife plunge down and put out a hand to protect Priya. But another hand shot out and grabbed Paul's wrist. It was Richard, and he fought with Paul, bending his arm backwards. The three men subdued Paul.

The helicopter was now directly overhead, the garish light from its search beam suddenly blinding, the thunder of its rotor blades deafening.

Rita pulled Priya to one side. The ropes tying her hands and ankles were too tight for Rita to remove. But she pulled off the cloth gag from her mouth. Priya dragged in a huge breath, then turned and retched on the ground.

Rizwan came over. He had a switchblade knife and cut the ropes while Rita urged Priya to remain still. The helicopter moved away, doing a circle around the scene.

"Is he… is he dead?" Priya asked, raising her head to watch the men restraining Paul.

"Unfortunately, no." Rita's voice was grim. "But he will spend the rest of his life behind bars. How are you?"

She held Priya's shoulders and looked at her. The woman dissolved into sobs, and Rita held her close.

"It's okay," she said. "You'll be safe now. And you helped us catch this man. You're very brave."

The men finished cuffing Paul, and Richard read him his rights. Hopkins came over to Rita.

"What shall we do, guv? Call the bird down for transport? The only problem is he can't land here."

"That's right. I don't think we need an airlift. It'll take us longer, but we can walk down to the car. Have you called for backup?"

"I'll do it now."

Rita pulled out her own radio and spoke to NPAS, who routed her through to the pilot.

"DI Gupta speaking," Rita said. "Ground situation under control. Can you please stay in patrol mode until we are in the cars?"

"Roger that," the pilot said.

The helicopter was distant now, but it made a low sweep and got closer again quickly. Rizwan and Hopkins held Paul by the scruff of the neck and made him walk.

"Feel free to smack him around if he stops walking," Rita said to Richard, who came over to speak to her. She lowered her voice. "But don't tell anyone I said that."

"No worries," Richard smiled and wiped the sweat from his face. "We intend to do exactly that."

The helicopter lit the way for them, and they used their torches again. It was a slow and painful walk, but at least they were going downhill now and visibility was better.

Rita and Priya got to the bottom of the hill first. They heard the wail of sirens, then the flashing blue lights appeared around the corner of the narrow Rosedale Chimney Bank road.

Rita sagged against the side of Rizwan's car. She still held Priya's hand as if she was afraid of losing her. Adrenaline bubbled in her veins as she watched the lights of a squad car and an ambulance get closer and then stop.

Rita was inside one of the cubicles at Scarborough General Hospital, and a doctor was shining a light in her eyes. She insisted she was fine, but they still did their checks. Priya was in the room next door. She had a laceration to her scalp, with some bleeding. She was getting stitches, but apart from that, she was free of major injury.

The curtains of the cubicle parted, and a familiar face peeked in. Jack Banford stepped inside and smiled at the doctor.

"He's my friend," Rita told the doctor. "Am I free to go now?"

The doctor nodded and stepped out of the cubicle. Jack's anxious eyes scanned her face.

"I came as soon as I heard from Mark Botley what happened. Are you okay?"

"Never been better," Rita grinned.

"I guess that was a stupid question. You got the guy, right? And saved the woman."

"Yes."

Jack massaged her shoulder, then pulled her into a hug. She succumbed to his embrace and suddenly felt intensely emotional. She choked back a sob, but teardrops leaked out. Jack held her tight.

"It's okay. You're human, alright?"

Rita separated from him and wiped her eyes angrily. "Sorry," she said. "That was unprofessional."

She accepted the tissue that Jack pulled from the dispenser on the wall and blew her nose.

She turned to Jack and sighed. "Thank you. And sorry about that again."

"Don't be," Jack said.

She saw something warm and fuzzy dance in his eyes, and she felt it too. But now was not the time or place to indulge in these things. She still had work to do.

"Let's check on Priya," she said.

They went outside and found Richard, Rizwan and Hopkins standing and chatting to Inspector Botley, with plastic cups of steaming coffee in their hands.

"Ey up, guv," Rizwan said, "you alright?"

"Yes," Rita said. "Any word on Priya? Where is she?"

Rizwan took her to a room with a door and knocked on it. A nurse opened the door and let them in.

Priya was awake, sitting up in bed. She looked exhausted, dark circles under her eyes.

Rita sat down by her bedside. She touched Priya's hand, and the woman gripped it tightly. Rita spoke to Jack and Rizwan. "Leave us for a bit. I'll see you outside."

She turned back to Priya after the door shut behind the men. "Tell me what happened."

"Paul... he was weird. Kind but strange. He said he wanted to take care of me. He got me a phone. I used it a couple of times to get in touch with my family. I did it from his van. Then he said he wanted to take me away. I wasn't sure, but what other choice did I have? It was better than the life I was living."

Priya stopped to drink some water. "When he came to the flat above the nail bar last night, he told me the plan. I was to meet him on a street in Eastfield, close to where we lived, at seven PM this evening."

"Did he drive the grey car?"

"Yes. Then we changed into the blue van."

Priya lapsed into silence. She didn't have to say the rest.

Rita said, "He took you to Rosedale, then overpowered you. Did he hurt you?"

"He gave me a drink, and I think it was drugged. I felt very sleepy. I was still awake when the van stopped, but then he hit me over the head when he dragged me out of the car. I don't remember much after that, apart from waking up on the cold hill."

Priya's eyes closed as her head lowered. Rita gripped her hand again. "Stay here. We will get in touch with your family first thing tomorrow. One of them will come here to take you home. Okay?"

Priya looked at Rita, and her eyes filled with tears. She couldn't speak.

Rita stood to leave, but Priya pulled on her hand.

"Thank you."

Rita smiled at her and went out.

Jack was waiting for her outside. He hung up on the phone call and took her to one side.

"You need to hear this. It's important."

CHAPTER 41

Jack dropped Rita off at home. Priya would stay in a custody cell overnight, where it was safest for her. Harper had called, asking for Priya to be handed over to the Modern Slavery Unit, but Rita had declined. She wanted to get more information from Priya about the trafficking gang. Harper told her he would come over as soon as he could tomorrow.

Rita had fallen into an exhausted, dreamless sleep. It was three in the morning when she finally slept, and yet the alarm still went off at its usual time of six a.m. She cursed as she awoke. She was still half-dressed from the waist up. She wanted nothing more than to carry on sleeping, but what Jack had told her came rushing back to her mind. Her eyelids flicked open, staring at the ceiling. She got up and dragged herself into the bathroom.

After half an hour, she twitched the curtains of her living room. Jack was outside, waiting in his car. They drove to the station, where Richard and Rizwan were waiting. They had already been debriefed. The research had been carried out, and Interpol had been alerted.

Rizwan had the Interpol reports ready. As Rita read the evidence, she had no doubt in her mind. She called DI Mansoor Ahmed in Bradford. He was happy to hear from her and updated her on the Yosef murder.

"Forensics didn't find a great deal. No fingerprints. Bleach was poured around the body, destroying any DNA evidence."

Rita smiled grimly. "And we don't have any CCTV evidence because the wires were cut. Convenient, isn't it?"

DI Ahmed hesitated, recognising the change in Rita's tone. "Sorry," he spoke slowly. "What do you mean?"

Rita told him. He listened in silence, then his voice shook. "Are you sure?"

"I can send you the documents from Interpol. We are en route, by the way. See you at the scene. We might need support. Is that okay?"

"I'll be there."

Rita hung up. She drove with Jack, while the lads led the way in an unmarked CID car. After an hour of driving at high speed, with their sirens on, they reached the outskirts of Leeds. Rizwan cut the sirens, and they drove slower as they entered the suburbs, finally arriving at their destination in the cul-de-sac. It was a normal residential area, with family homes, trimmed green front lawns, and white fences.

Rita was in radio contact with DI Ahmed. She heard his voice crackling through the static.

"My units are in place. Do you want an AFO?"
Authorised Firearms Officer.

"No," Rita said quietly. "It should be okay. I have my team."

"Be careful," DI Ahmed warned. "My team are ready to move in. Are you sure you don't want us to go first?"

"No," Rita said firmly. She got out of the car. So did Jack, and she turned to him.

"You can't go in there."

"I think I should."

Richard and Rizwan walked over from their car. Jack glanced at them. "I think we should go in together."

Rita had to make a quick decision. They couldn't stand out here, drawing attention. She nodded at Jack.

"OK, come with me. But you two, break and enter at the first hint of trouble."

Rizwan and Richard nodded. They went back to their car. Rita walked up to the house and knocked on the front door.

After a few seconds, a man in a bathrobe opened the door.

Inspector James Harper was surprised to see them.

"Rita? What're you doing here?" His eyes flicked to Jack, then slowly back to Rita.

"Who's this?"

"My friend, Jack Banford. He's a solicitor."

"Okay," Harper said slowly. "What's going on?" He glanced past Rita's shoulder, checking the street outside.

A woman's voice came from inside, and then a short blonde woman appeared, dressed in jeans and a jumper.

"James? Who's at the door?"

"Just some colleagues from work. I'll speak to them."

The woman smiled at Rita. "Hi." She didn't offer her name.

Rita smiled back and stepped inside. Harper didn't like it—she could tell. He was stiff and glaring at Jack as he walked in.

"The study's here," he said, walking down the hallway. He passed the living room and turned left before the open-plan kitchen and dining area. Rita noted the expensive marble floor, the granite kitchen countertops, and the high-end brand of kitchen appliances. Beyond the glass concertina doors, a neat garden stretched out, flanked by mature trees at the back.

Harper opened the study door and ushered them in. "Have a seat," he indicated the sofa opposite the desk.

"I'll stand," Rita said.

"Me too," Jack confirmed.

"OK," Harper frowned, drawing out the words. "What's going on?"

"You've done well for yourself on a police officer's salary," Rita said, pointing at the expensive original artwork on the walls. She turned back to Harper.

"Where were you yesterday?"

"I was at the head office in Leeds. I told you. Then I came over to Bradford when you called me."

Rita said, "Your boss is Inspector Ridley Garth, correct?"

Harper narrowed his eyes. "Yes. Why do you ask?"

Rita glanced at Jack. "Mr Garth is friends with the partner of our law firm in Bradford. I contacted the partner, who is my colleague, obviously. I did so because I remembered a case of an inspector from the Modern Slavery Unit being investigated by the Anti-Corruption Unit."

Harper's face changed. "Oh, that. All charges were dropped against me. Is that what you came here for?"

His shoulders relaxed as he leaned against the door. Rita noted they were standing in the middle of the room, but James had placed himself by the door, which he hadn't locked.

She said, "Your boss didn't see you yesterday. Jack's colleague was actually at the MSU HQ. No one had seen you in the office. Where were you?"

"I was there," Harper frowned. "And I did see people."

Rita ignored him. "Your car was picked up on ANPR. It was on the road to Bradford, and then it vanished in a dark spot. Later, CCTV shows another car entering the private estate where Yosef Musa lived. The plates of the car show it to be a rental vehicle—one rented by a company that you own. You're the sole director of," Rita pulled out her phone and read from the screen, "New Horizon Property Renovations. Is that correct?"

Harper was still as a statue. "That's not true."

"But it is, and you know it. You broke into Yosef Musa's house. You knew where the cables were. You cut them and then waited for him to come back."

"This is nonsense," Harper said, shaking his head. A muscle ticked in his jaw. "I can't believe I'm hearing this."

Jack said, "The charges the ACU made against you were dropped, but they renewed their case when CCTV showed you meeting with Yosef Musa. That's the new case my partner is involved in. As part of the prosecution, they've contacted Interpol, who have video evidence of you meeting with other human trafficking gang suspects in Amsterdam, Málaga, and Athens. Three months ago, you were also seen in Mumbai."

Rita said, "And we have all the evidence in our possession." She paused, fixing Harper with a glare. "You left Scarborough early yesterday because you wanted to come back and kill Yosef. You were the reason the police never got hold of Rafik. He was always alerted in advance. You have a thriving business because your gang always stays out of the law's reach."

"I don't have time for this," Harper snarled. His cheeks were red, and a vein throbbed in his forehead.

He turned the door handle and rushed out. Then he stopped abruptly.

Richard and Rizwan were standing there. Behind them, DI Ahmed stood, his mouth open in disbelief, his cheeks mottled with anger.

"You swine," DI Ahmed shouted. "We dropped so many investigations because of you. All along, you were playing us. I put my career on the line listening to your crap." He brushed past Richard and lunged for Harper, but Rizwan restrained him.

Rita said, "James Harper, you're under arrest for human trafficking. You don't have to say anything, but anything you do say can be used against you in a court of law."

Rizwan pushed Harper against the wall while DI Ahmed snapped the cuffs on him.

His girlfriend appeared, shouting and upset. "What's going on?"

Harper stared at Rita with glassy, lifeless eyes.

"Take him to the car," Rita ordered.

CHAPTER 42

His Majesty's Prison Full Sutton was about forty miles southeast of Scarborough, housing some of the UK's most dangerous prisoners. It was a designated Category A and B men's prison—one of the most highly secure in the country.

It was where Edward Kyle Warren was incarcerated. He lay in his cell, hands folded under his head, staring at the ceiling.

No, he wasn't sorry for what he'd done. He had enjoyed abducting that boy, and his only mistake had been not killing his partner, Stuart, earlier. Stuart had given the game away. If it hadn't been for him, Ed would've been far away by now, enjoying a glass of sangria in sunny Málaga. As for the boy, he would've got used to his new life. He didn't exactly have a choice.

That would've been nice. Ed liked young boys. He liked young girls too, and women. But he was going through a phase of enjoying boys. It was a shame that had come to an end so abruptly, he thought to himself.

His jaw hardened when he thought of that bitch, Detective Inspector Rita Gupta. Who the hell did she think she was? How dare she spoil his fun?

Ed's lawyer had assured him that he had to show good behaviour, be nice to the guards, and keep his nose clean. He hadn't been sentenced yet. The court case was still two months away. Until then, he would be kept here. If he got a lighter sentence at the hearing, he might be moved to a less secure Category C or D prison. Then he'd get privileges like daily phone calls, hot drinks, and meeting with other inmates in the play area.

But here, he got nothing but solitary confinement and a guard outside his door. His lawyer had told him that DI Rita Gupta had made sure he was sent to the highest-security prison.

Why?

Because of Detective Constable Maggie Long.

Ed closed his eyes, and Maggie's lovely face swam into his vision. The blonde curls of her hair, shining in the sun. The dazzle in her blue eyes as she smiled at him. She was in love, he could tell. She was much younger than him, and he had enjoyed her youthful body. He hadn't wanted much more, though, but she had other plans. She went and got herself pregnant, didn't she?

Ed shook his head. He should never have trusted a woman. He had used a condom. Had the bitch put a hole in it? Is that how she got pregnant? Ed had a naturally suspicious mind, and he wouldn't put it past Maggie.

The viewing bar on the door slid open.

"It's time," the guard said through the open bar. Ed could see the man's eyes through the slit.

The guard spoke again. "Stand back and put your hands up in the air. Stay like that till we come in. Got it?"

"Yes," Ed said resignedly.

He got out of bed. The guard watched him, then two of them entered. One patted him down while the other stood behind him. Then one of them searched his room while the other kept watch. Ed had to keep his hands behind his head.

Then they snapped handcuffs on him.

When he first arrived here, he had been allowed hot drinks, but he had spat one at a guard. From then on, he had to wear a mouth guard and lost his privileges. He regretted that. It was awful not getting hot coffee in the morning.

The mouth guard was fastened, and then he was marched out of the room.

They walked down the corridor and stopped at a metal gate, where they were buzzed into another corridor. This led to the reception office with its steel-reinforced glass frontage. Ed was taken inside, and after another short walk through another set of doors, he was shown into the viewing chamber.

Here, he was searched once again, and then his handcuffs and mouth guard were removed.

His sister sat in the visitor's room, and her eyes lit up when she saw him. She stood, and he went over and kissed her on the cheek.

Luna had brown hair that looked newly cut. She smelt of cigarettes and cheap perfume. Her makeup was overdone, her cheeks so red they could stop cars at a traffic light. Her lips were fattened with dermal fillers. She had the fake eyelashes too, and with her duck lips, she looked like a glossy magazine's idea of a trashy celebrity.

"How could they do this to yer?" Luna whined in her high-pitched voice. "I can't believe it, tho."

"I need to get out of here," Ed said. "This place is killing me."

"And what about your child? You need to see him, don't you? Or her. You know you can get compassionate leave for that, don't you? Ask your lawyer."

"Right." Ed narrowed his eyes. "Who told you?"

"When Brian was in jail, he got out on parole to see Ginny."

Brian was one of the fathers of Luna's five children. She had at least three different fathers for her kids.

"I think you can get out to see your child. You should ask them."

Ed nodded slowly. He thought of Maggie, and he knew she would want to keep the child.

Could that be his way out of here?

A sudden plan started to form in his mind.

He leaned forward and lowered his voice. "I've got a score to settle with that Detective Inspector who arrested me and the mother of my child. They can't keep me here. I've done nothing wrong."

Luna held his gaze.

"I'm listening, bruv. Carry on."

"Her name is Inspector Rita Gupta. She's based in Scarborough. That bitch is the reason I ended up here. I should be in a less secure prison."

Luna had a frown on her face. She was staring at her brother intently. Ed said, "What?"

"What's the name of that inspector again?"

"Rita Gupta."

Luna froze and her eyes widened. She swore loudly, and the guard glanced at them. "Keep your voice down," Ed said. He was intrigued by Luna's reaction. "What's the matter?"

"I know that name. You know my new man, Rafik?"

Ed shrugged. Luna went through men like she was shredding old bills; he couldn't keep count. He didn't tell her that because she'd get offended. Luna pouted with her duck lips, and made a funny sound in her throat. She put her elbows on the table and leaned forward.

"He's my new fella. I told yer about him but you forgotten now. He's Indian, like originally, you know. Anyway, he got into some trouble with the cops. For no reason, they're hassling him. He's got a few kids over from India on a student visa – that's his business, he arranges their education. Puts them in a college, and keeps a few bob for himself. Nice little earner. But now the cops think some of the kids are illegal immigrants. Honestly – it's total crap. Rafik's a good man. Bloody pigs, eh?"

Ed was listening with growing interest. "Carry on."

"So he was saying this female Inspector called Rita Gupta was chasing after him. She was making his life hell. So bad that he's gone away for a couple of weeks. I'm still in touch with him, like. Listen, you keep this to yourself, okay?"

"Of course. So this Rafik of yours, he hates Rita Gupta, right?"

"Yes. He's found out where she lives. He was thinking of putting a brick through her window. But that won't get him owt."

Ed was thinking fast. He could use Rafik against Rita. And he knew just the way to do it. But first, he had to get to Molly, and his child. That child would be his way out of prison. But it was important for Rafik to remain outside prison, too.

He dropped his voice to a whisper. "Listen to me, sis. Listen very carefully."

Want to know what happens next?

Carry on reading in Book 5 – *I Know You Lied*

Author's Note

Like a plant, a book is born in silence and isolation. It's air, water and sustenance is you – the reader.

When a reader leaves a review, the little sapling rises in the air, and someday, bears leaves and flowers.

If you can, please leave a review on Amazon, Goodreads, wherever you can. This humble self-published author will appreciate it immensely.

Please search on Amazon for The Broken Souls by Sam Carter.

Many thanks
Sam.

Printed in Great Britain
by Amazon